W9-CDL-508

She would once again have a Cinderella night with her very own Prince Charming.

But the difference between herself and fairy-tale Cindy was that the prince would not be showing up at her door once he learned Margaret's secret.

No, Gibson McKinley wouldn't elect to keep company with a woman who had to hire a baby-sitter before she could venture out on a date. Gib had finished his stint of late-night feedings and chicken pox years ago.

So this night, Margaret mused, was her grand finale. She was fortunate to have been granted one last night with Gib before she became a mommy again. And she'd savor every moment, every memory made....

Tux, Bram, Blue and Gib
are four unforgettable men with love as
endless as the Texas sky, just waiting for
women special enough to win their hearts!

Dear Reader,

The holiday season has arrived—and we have some dazzling titles for the month of December!

This month, the always-delightful Joan Elliott Pickart brings you our THAT'S MY BABY! title. *Texas Baby* is the final book in her FAMILY MEN cross-line series with Desire, and spins the heartwarming tale of a fortysomething heroine who rediscovers the joy of motherhood when she adopts a precious baby girl. Except the dashing man of her dreams has no intention of playing daddy again....

And baby fever doesn't stop there. Don't miss *The Littlest Angel* by Sherryl Woods, an emotional reunion romance—and the first of her AND BABY MAKES THREE: THE NEXT GENERATION miniseries. Passion flares between a disgruntled cowboy and a tough lady cop in *The Cop and the Cradle* by Suzannah Davis—book two in the SWITCHED AT BIRTH miniseries.

For those of you who revel in holiday miracles, be sure to check out *Christmas Magic* by Andrea Edwards. This humorous romance features a cat-toting heroine who transforms a former Mr. Scrooge into a true believer—and captures his heart in the process.

Also this month, *The Millionaire's Baby* by Phyllis Halldorson is an absorbing amnesia story that's filled with love, turmoil and a possible second chance at happiness. Finally, long-buried feelings resurface when a heroine returns to unite her former lover with the son he'd never known in *Second Chance Dad* by Angela Benson.

All of us here at Silhouette wish you a joyous holiday season!

Sincerely,

Tara Gavin,
Senior Editor

Please address questions and book requests to:
Silhouette Reader Service
U.S.: 3010 Walden Ave., P.O. Box 1325, Buffalo, NY 14269
Canadian: P.O. Box 609, Fort Erie, Ont. L2A 5X3

JOAN ELLIOTT PICKART

TEXAS BABY

Silhouette®

SPECIAL ▼ EDITION®

Published by Silhouette Books

America's Publisher of Contemporary Romance

If you purchased this book without a cover you should be aware
that this book is stolen property. It was reported as "unsold and
destroyed" to the publisher, and neither the author nor the
publisher has received any payment for this "stripped book."

For Autumn's "morning family":
Tish, Brian, Aubree and Taylor
with love and hugs and oodles of thanks

 SILHOUETTE BOOKS

ISBN 0-373-24141-0

TEXAS BABY

Copyright © 1997 by Joan Elliott Pickart

All rights reserved. Except for use in any review, the reproduction
or utilization of this work in whole or in part in any form by any
electronic, mechanical or other means, now known or hereafter
invented, including xerography, photocopying and recording, or in
any information storage or retrieval system, is forbidden without
the written permission of the editorial office, Silhouette Books,
300 East 42nd Street, New York, NY 10017 U.S.A.

All characters in this book have no existence outside the imagination of
the author and have no relation whatsoever to anyone bearing the same
name or names. They are not even distantly inspired by any individual
known or unknown to the author, and all incidents are pure invention.

This edition published by arrangement with Harlequin Books S.A.

® and TM are trademarks of Harlequin Books S.A., used under license.
Trademarks indicated with ® are registered in the United States Patent
and Trademark Office, the Canadian Trade Marks Office and in other
countries.

Printed in U.S.A.

Books by Joan Elliott Pickart

Silhouette Special Edition

*Friends, Lovers...and Babies! #1011
*The Father of Her Child #1025
†Texas Dawn #1100
†Texas Baby #1141

*The Baby Bet
†Family Men

Silhouette Desire

*Angels and Elves #961
Apache Dream Bride #999
†Texas Moon #1051
†Texas Glory #1088

Previously published under the pseudonym Robin Elliott

Silhouette Desire

Call It Love #213
To Have It All #237
Picture of Love #261
Pennies in the Fountain #275
Dawn's Gift #303
Brooke's Chance #323
Betting Man #344
Silver Sands #362
Lost and Found #440
Out of the Cold #440
Sophie's Attic #725
Not Just Another Perfect Wife #818
Haven's Call #859

Silhouette Special Edition

Rancher's Heaven #909
Mother at Heart #968

Silhouette Intimate Moments

Gauntlet Run #206

JOAN ELLIOTT PICKART

is the author of over seventy novels. When she isn't writing, she enjoys watching football, knitting, reading, gardening and attending craft shows on the town square. Joan has three all-grown-up daughters and a fantastic little grandson. In September of 1995 Joan traveled to China to adopt her fourth daughter, three-month-old Autumn. Joan and Autumn have settled into their cozy cottage in a charming small town in the high pine country of Arizona.

Dear Reader,

When I introduced Margaret Madison in *Texas Dawn* (Special Edition #1100), I knew she was a special woman who had a story to tell.

As *Texas Baby* unfolded, I felt a bond with Margaret, as though we had been friends for a very long time. As a single mother, I had adopted a wonderful baby girl from China after raising three daughters. My precious Autumn is to me the miracle that Alison is to Margaret.

But Margaret's life became more complex than mine, with the emergence of Gibson McKinley into her serene existence with her new daughter.

I cordially invite you to travel the journey to true love with Margaret and Gib. Laugh with them, cry with them and finally rejoice in their happiness. It's a bumpy trip for this couple as they make their way forward, so settle in for a roller-coaster ride to sweet bliss.

I sincerely hope you enjoy *Texas Baby*.

Warmest regards,

Joan Elliott Pickart

Prologue

"Well, I declare, if this isn't just fine, havin' you come to visit your ole Granny Bee. You sit yourself right down here, 'cause this is porch-sittin' weather.

"You get yourself comfy and I'll tell you a story, just as I promised I would the last time you came to call.

"Now, you know that all three of the Bishop boys are married and mighty happy 'bout it. They all found their forever love, just as they were hopin' to do.

"Well, as I was hintin' to you before, there were some other folks who were in for some mighty big changes in their lives. They just didn't know it yet.

"Remember me tellin' you how that fella Gibson McKinley and Margaret Madison seemed to get on just fine together at Blue and Amy's weddin'? Margaret is Amy's mother, if you recall, and Gib owns *The Houston Holler* newspaper.

"Anyway, folks were wonderin' whether Margaret and Gibson might start spendin' time together, seein' how they'd danced only with each other at Blue and Amy's weddin' reception.

"I was watchin' 'em that night, you know, and thinkin' there was somethin' special happenin' between 'em.

"But, well, people are so busy in this world these days and don't always hear what their heart might be whisperin' to 'em, 'cause they got a long list of what needs doin' chatterin' in their minds.

"That's how it was with Gibson McKinley and Margaret Madison, their bein' busy and all. So, the love bee—I truly believe the love bug is a bee, you understand, 'cause I got my name of Granny Bee from making honey from all my sweet, darlin' bees—well, the love bee just sometimes has to nudge folks a tad to get 'em movin' in the direction they were meant to be goin'.

"And that's just what happened one day when Margaret was downtown shoppin' and Gibson was spendin' lunchtime buyin' some new shirts.

"Gib and Margaret didn't realize it, but they were in the same store, not more than a dozen feet or so apart.

"So, that love bee got to buzzin', and the next thing you know..."

Chapter One

Margaret Madison was glancing at a dress displayed on a mannequin in the department store when she turned the corner at the perfume counter. In the next instant she collided with something very solid. She gasped in surprise and dropped her packages.

"Oh, dear." She looked up quickly, only to have another little gasp escape her lips. "Gibson! *You're* the wall I bumped into? I'm terribly sorry."

"Hello, Margaret," he said, smiling. "There's no damage done. Let me help you gather your belongings before someone steps on them."

Margaret turned away to begin collecting the scattered shopping bags.

Gibson McKinley. She hadn't seen him since Amy and Blue's wedding. She and Gibson had danced every dance together at the reception, and the entire evening had been perfect.

She'd watched her precious daughter marry the man who had captured Amy's heart forever. How beautiful her Amy had been, such a lovely, glowing bride.

Blue Bishop had been a picture-perfect groom, as well, appearing as though he'd just stepped off the top of the wedding cake.

And she, herself, had been made to feel special, lovely, young and very feminine, during the hours spent dancing in the strong arms of tall, handsome and charming Gibson McKinley.

She'd anticipated Gibson's call over the following days, rushing to answer the telephone every time it rang, acting like a silly schoolgirl. But there hadn't been a call. She hadn't heard one word from Gibson since that Cinderella night nearly three months before.

She had been simply a means by which Gibson could fill the social hours of a wedding reception, she'd finally decided with a flash of anger. He hadn't given her a second thought since that night.

Margaret finally straightened and accepted the two packages that Gibson had retrieved.

"Thank you," she said. "I apologize again for not watching where I was going. Have a nice day, Gibson. Goodbye."

"Margaret, wait a minute," Gibson said. "Do you have to rush off? Would you care to join me for lunch? I ducked out of the office to buy some shirts and I haven't eaten yet. The little restaurant down the block has excellent food. What do you say?''

What *should* she say? Margaret thought. She was definitely "out of sight, out of mind" to this man. And now that he'd caught sight of her again, he was oozing charm and attention.

Well, forget it, Mr. McKinley.

But the memories of those fairy-tale hours spent with Gibson had refused to leave her alone, stealing too frequently into her dreams at night and popping up with annoying regularity during the day.

Perhaps she *would* have lunch with him, view him under normal circumstances far removed from the nostalgic, romantic atmosphere of a wedding. Then she would be able to close the book on Gibson McKinley, playboy extraordinaire of Houston, Texas.

"All right, Gibson," she said, smiling slightly as she lifted her chin. "Lunch sounds like a fine idea."

"Fantastic. May I carry your parcels, ma'am?"

"No, no, I'll manage to hang on to them this time. Shall we go?"

Gibson stepped back to allow Margaret to move ahead of him in the crowded store, the crunch of people making it impossible for him to walk by her side as they made their way slowly toward the front doors.

Margaret Madison. He swept his gaze over her, the sight of her slender figure, her short, wavy strawberry-blond hair, the sway of her gently sloping hips bringing back vivid memories of the hours he'd spent holding her in his arms as they danced at Blue and Amy's wedding reception.

For the first time in probably over thirty years, the image of a woman had haunted him beyond the time he'd actually spent with her. He'd remembered Margaret's big, expressive brown eyes and lovely features, her delicate aroma of flowers, the sound of her lilting laughter, the velvet caress of her voice.

And, oh, yes, he thought dryly, he definitely recalled time and again how her body had felt pressed to his as they'd danced the night away. He'd spent more than one night in the past three months tossing and turning, his body heated and aroused because of Margaret Madison.

Like a nervous adolescent, he'd telephoned Margaret the day after the wedding with the intention of asking her out to dinner. He'd let the telephone ring twenty times before admitting reluctantly that she wasn't home. Over the next two weeks he'd called six—or was it seven?—times, only to have the unanswered ringing echo in his ear.

Margaret Madison was one busy lady, he'd finally concluded, surprised by his reaction of anger and disappointment. A lady with a long line of admirers on the hook, no doubt. Well, he had no intention of taking a number and waiting his turn to keep company with Mrs. Madison.

So why had he invited her to lunch? The words had spilled out of his mouth before he'd known he was going to say them. And even more puzzling and ridiculous was the elation he'd felt when Margaret agreed to join him for the meal.

Oh, well. Gibson mentally sighed. He'd spend an hour or so with Margaret over lunch, and that would be that. It was actually a good move, the more he thought about it. A safe, sedate lunch would replace the memories of the wedding reception. There would be no more sleepless nights looming in his future.

The air outside the automatic doors was hot and heavy, compared to the near chill of the department store.

Gibson was able to inch his way next to Margaret despite the bustling mass of people on the sidewalk. But conversation was impossible as they hurried along, eager to enter the air-conditioned restaurant.

Once they were inside, the attractive hostess greeted them with a smile.

"Hello, Gib," she said. "It's good to see you. I thought you'd forgotten we're still here, serving the best food in Houston."

"I would never forget you, Anna," Gibson said, smiling. "Do you have a table for two available?"

"For you? Yes. Follow me, please."

Margaret resisted the urge to roll her eyes heavenward as Anna led them to a table in the far corner that overlooked a pretty, glass-enclosed patio edged with vibrant flowers.

Gibson had pushed his charisma button, Margaret thought, and voilà, a table was ready for him, despite the fact that at least half a dozen people were standing in the entryway of the restaurant waiting to be seated. Mr. McKinley certainly didn't hesitate in using his handsome good looks to his advantage.

Stop it, she scolded herself. Why was she being so critical, so quick to find fault with Gibson? It wasn't even close to being her normal behavior.

Admit it, Margaret. Her feminine ego had taken a blow when she hadn't heard from Gibson after the wondrous night of dancing at the wedding reception. Well, that was no excuse for being witchy.

She'd have lunch with Gibson McKinley, chalk up further evidence that he wasn't Prince Charming from the Cinderella evening they'd shared, and put him out of her mind once and for all. While doing so, she would be her usual polite and pleasant self.

Gibson assisted Margaret with her chair, then sat opposite her. After Margaret stacked her packages on the floor beside her, Anna handed them menus, said a waiter would be along in a moment and told Gibson once again how good it was to see him.

"You must eat here often," Margaret said after Anna had disappeared from view.

"No, I don't get over here all that much," Gibson answered. "I usually don't have time for a lengthy lunch. Have you been here before?"

Margaret nodded, then glanced around the room before looking at Gibson again.

"This place has a quiet elegance that is a peaceful respite in a busy day. The tablecloths, flowers and candles, the waiters in tuxedos…it all makes me feel pampered and special."

Gibson smiled. "Nicely put. I can see where Amy

gets her flair for choosing just the right words to use in her writing. Your daughter is an excellent reporter. I'm glad she's still taking assignments from me for *The Holler*, now that she's a freelance journalist.''

"She didn't inherit her writing ability from me," Margaret said, laughing. "She got that from her father. As I told you the night of Amy and Blue's wedding, my forte is music. More precisely, the piano."

"Margaret," Gibson began, a serious expression on his face, "I'm glad you brought up that night. I—"

"Good afternoon," a man in a tuxedo said, suddenly appearing at the table. "Are you ready to order?"

Margaret and Gib looked quickly at their menus.

"I'll have a Caesar salad and iced tea, please," Margaret said.

"Baked trout," Gibson said, "and coffee."

The waiter nodded, collected their menus and hurried away.

Margaret spread her napkin on her lap, sliding a glance at Gibson in the process.

He really was ruggedly handsome, she mused. Her memories of him had been right on the mark. His features were rough-hewn and masculine. His eyes were very dark, as was his hair, which boasted distinguished-looking streaks of gray at the temples.

And she knew, from spending hours dancing in his arms, that his six-foot body was taut and nicely muscled. It was no wonder that Gibson McKinley had been voted one of Houston's top-ten eligible bachelors for the past five years. Being the wealthy owner of *The Houston Holler* didn't hurt his credentials, either.

"Margaret?"

She blinked as the sound of Gibson speaking her name brought her back to attention.

"I'm sorry," she said. "I was woolgathering."

He'd had no intention of pursuing the subject of the night he and Margaret had met. But he'd certainly been doing exactly that when the waiter had interrupted him, he chided himself. He didn't want to talk about that evening, because it might lead to his revealing that he'd made endless attempts to contact Margaret during the following days. He wasn't about to set his bruised ego on the table to take another punch.

"You've obviously been extremely busy during the past weeks," he said.

Margaret frowned slightly. "Obviously? Why would you draw that conclusion?"

"Oh, well, what I meant was..." Gibson paused and shook his head. "The hell with it. Margaret, I telephoned you so many times after the night of the wedding, I could have dialed your number with my eyes closed. You were never home."

A strange warmth suffused Margaret, and a funny flutter danced along her spine.

Gibson *had* called her after that incredible evening? Had, in fact, telephoned time and again? All these weeks she'd assumed that he... He could have dialed her number with his eyes closed?

Margaret, please, she thought. To use Amy's vernacular, get a grip. So Gibson's news flash was an unexpected and pleasant surprise that certainly soothed her wounded ego, but, heavens, there was no reason to go off the deep end. What was next? She'd leap onto the table and shout ''hooray'' at the top of her lungs?

''I'm sorry I missed your calls, Gibson,'' she said. Did her voice sound weird, sort of breathy, wobbly? Good grief, she hoped not.

''And that's another thing,'' Gibson said, frowning. ''You're still referring to me as Gibson. As I told you the night we met, all my friends call me Gib.''

''And as I replied that night,'' Margaret said, smiling, ''I'm one of those old-fashioned people who doesn't take the title of 'friend' lightly. The majority of those surrounding me are acquaintances.''

Gibson nodded. ''Yes, I remember you saying that. I was going to ask you what a person had to do to earn the privilege of being your friend, but someone interrupted us at that moment and I lost my train of thought. So, I'm asking you now.''

''I used to have a long list. You know, a friend likes you even if you're having a grumpy day, things such as that. Then Amy asked me for my definition when she was at an age when she couldn't sit still and certainly didn't want a sermon on the subject. I cut it back to short and sweet.''

''And?''

''A friend is someone you could telephone at two

in the morning, say 'I need you,' and they'd come, without asking why.''

Gibson studied her for a long moment, as though he were seeing her for the first time.

What a classy woman, he thought. Margaret Madison was not only extremely attractive—beautiful, really—she also had class.

During the evening they'd spent together he'd discovered that she was intelligent, had a sense of humor, was strong and independent while being gentle and womanly.

And now he knew she had class, grace and dignity, values he respected. Her definition of a friend might sound simplistic, but to him it had depth beyond measure.

Margaret hadn't said a friend would give her their last dollar, or loan her their new car. She hadn't touched on the materialistic at all. She simply wanted to know that her friend would be there for her if she needed him, no questions asked.

He liked that. He liked that very, very much.

"Margaret," he said, looking directly into her brown eyes, "I'd be honored if you'd call me Gib. I'd like to believe that we're friends. I *would* come at two in the morning if you needed me, and I wouldn't ask why."

"Thank you…Gib," Margaret said softly.

They smiled at each other—warm smiles, gentle smiles, smiles that were important and marked the passing of a hurdle, smiles of understanding and a modicum of trust.

The smiles faded slowly, changed, as the man saw the woman, the woman saw the man. The noise in the restaurant faded into oblivion. Desire curled and swirled around them, into them, low and pulsing, creating such heat.

They were dancing again, held fast in each other's arms, bodies pressed close, swaying to the music being played just for them. She was Cinderella and he was Prince Charming, and the clock was *never* going to strike midnight.

"Your salad, madam," the waiter said.

Margaret jumped in surprise at the sudden intrusion, then fiddled with the napkin on her lap as the waiter placed the food on the table.

Dear heaven, she thought, what had happened? How much time had passed? It was as though a magical and sensuous spell had been cast over her and Gibson and—no, he was Gib. His name was Gib McKinley, because he would come to her at two in the morning if she needed him, and he wouldn't ask why.

Gib was her friend.

And that fact was something she knew she would treasure.

He was also a man, who was making her incredibly aware, once again, of her own femininity. She'd felt the fire of desire the night of the wedding and again just moments ago, womanly desire she'd believed had been extinguished when her husband, Jack, had died.

This was all so frightening. But yet, it was exciting, too, to feel so vibrantly alive, so in tune with her own body. She was Margaret Madison, who was forty-six years...young. She knew who she was, what she was and why she was. At that very moment she was in the company of a dynamic, charming, handsome man, and she intended to enjoy every second of it.

Margaret sampled the large salad in front of her.

"Delicious," she said, smiling. "How's your trout...Gib?"

"What? Oh, it's fine, very good."

It was? Gib thought dryly. He'd taken a couple of bites of the fish and hadn't tasted a thing, hardly remembered chewing and swallowing.

Margaret was having a potent effect on him, that was for sure. For a moment there—or had it been an hour?—he had been consumed with heated desire.

And memories. He'd *felt* Margaret's slender body nestled against him as they danced. He was positive that during the strange interlude that had just transpired, he had inhaled her aroma of flowers, savored the sensation of her silky hair on his cheek.

This woman, who was now blissfully eating her giant salad, was a spell weaver. He was not, he knew, going to be able to dismiss her from his mind when their lunch together was over.

Well, so be it. It wouldn't cause a problem to see Margaret socially for a while. They enjoyed each other's company, and heaven knew there was a sexual attraction between them.

He'd been working long hours lately, and hadn't

dated anyone for weeks. It was time to play a bit. As long as he remained fully aware that Margaret got to him by simply being her honest, open and real self, he wouldn't fall prey to anything beyond the physical chemistry that sizzled and crackled between them.

There. He had it all squared away. Now maybe he could actually taste his lunch. He'd also better tune back in to the conversation, because Margaret was speaking to him and he hadn't heard a word she was saying.

"...absolutely lovely," Margaret said. "It's a shame you missed Glory and Bram's wedding. Amy told me you were in New York for some kind of newspaper convention, or some such thing."

"Yes, I was," Gib said, nodding. "I was sorry I couldn't attend the wedding of the last of the Bishop boys. Their mother, Jana-John, and I have been friends for many years. Their father, too, of course. But Jana-John and I go back to before she married Abe."

"Well, my Amy is certainly all aglow with the Bishop she married. When I see Amy and Blue together, I can actually feel the love between them. It's every mother's dream to have her child find that kind of happiness. Forever love is what Blue calls it. Speaking of children, your daughter is content with her life, isn't she?"

"Betsy? Oh, yes, she certainly is. She has two fantastic kids and a fine man for a husband. I thoroughly enjoy being a grandfather." Gib laughed. "You know that old saying about being a grandparent. You can spoil the grandchildren rotten, then go home to peace and quiet, leaving the parents to deal with the monsters.''

"You…need…peace and quiet?" Margaret said, no hint of a smile on her face.

"After a long day at *The Holler*, the silence of my house is music to my ears. I've been a widower for over seven years. I'm used to the lack of noise and confusion at home.''

"I see," Margaret said.

Gib frowned. "Did I miss something here? You're suddenly so serious, as though I said I went home after work and buried bodies in the basement.''

"No, no," Margaret said quickly. "You didn't miss anything. What you said is perfectly reasonable. People our age usually relish the quietness of the empty nest.''

"Usually? Meaning you don't?"

"I didn't say that. Would you hand me the salt, please?"

Gib gave Margaret the saltshaker she could easily have reached herself.

"Margaret," he said, "I have the feeling we're playing word games, skittering around something, but not really addressing it.''

That is very astute, Mr. McKinley, Margaret thought, but she had no intention of discussing the subject they were skittering around, as he put it. Not here. Not now. Not yet.

Her secret was still tucked safely and carefully in her heart, known only to herself and a few others.

Her own daughter wasn't aware of her mother's dream. She would tell Amy soon, very soon, but she certainly wasn't confiding in Gib at this point.

"Your journalistic mind is working overtime," Margaret said, producing a small smile. "So! Tell me about your trip to New York. Was it all work, or did you have an opportunity to do the town? See some Broadway shows? Go to museums?"

Nice try, Margaret, Gib thought. She was definitely hiding something, steering the conversation away from a subject she didn't want to talk about.

Her strange behavior had begun when he'd said some inane thing about welcoming the peace and quiet at home after a day at *The Holler.*

What on earth was this intriguing woman keeping from him?

"Gib? New York?"

"Oh, yes, the Big Apple. Like a lot of people, I feel it's a fun place to visit, but I wouldn't want to live there. I'd never get used to the hustle and bustle. I can't figure out why everyone is always in such a hurry to get where they're going." Gib laughed. "Of course, I *am* going to celebrate my fiftieth birthday this year. Maybe I'm too old to take on the franticness of Manhattan."

"You don't honestly believe that fifty is old, do you?" Margaret said.

Gib shrugged. "I don't know. I haven't really given it any thought."

"I was forty-six a couple of months ago. I, for one, feel very young, excited about life and the future. Age is just a number. It's how we perceive ourselves, how we live that's important.''

"Yes, ma'am," Gib said, smiling. "I understand, ma'am."

Margaret blushed a pretty pink. "I'm sorry. I didn't mean to get on my soapbox. It's just that... Oh, never mind. You were telling me about New York."

Gib stared at Margaret for a long moment, wishing he could peer into her pretty head, get a clue about what she *wasn't* divulging.

Maybe Margaret was right. Maybe his years as a journalist caused him to continually overreact, to always be on the alert for the message beneath the surface. But in the case of Margaret Madison, he didn't think he was off track. The lady had a secret she was keeping to herself.

And the newsperson within him—and, yes, the man—wanted to know what it was. Now, however, he'd be foolish to push. Margaret was on the alert and skillfully redirecting the topic of the conversation.

The meal was concluded with pleasant chitchat, and with a sense of reluctance Gib finally said he had to return to the office for a meeting. The lunch *hour* shared with Margaret had swiftly become two.

On the sidewalk in front of the restaurant, Margaret thanked Gib for the meal and his company.

"The pleasure was mine, I assure you," Gib said, then paused. "Listen, this is Tuesday. Miss Manners would agree that I'm being socially correct and asking far enough in advance if you'd have dinner with me Saturday night?''

Margaret hesitated for a moment, then smiled. ''Yes, I'd like that.''

''Good. Seven o'clock?''

Margaret nodded, still smiling. They parted, going in opposite directions.

It wasn't until he was back in the office that Gib realized, with a burst of laughter, that he'd totally forgotten to buy new shirts.

Chapter Two

The Madison family home was a four-bedroom ranch-style. Years before, one of the bedrooms had been converted into a library-cum-office, where Jack Madison had spent many hours concentrating on work he'd brought home from the office.

The living room had a fireplace surrounded by flagstones and topped with a mantel that held a vast array of framed family pictures. A baby grand piano had a place of honor in the corner of the large room.

Instead of drapes, Margaret had chosen shutters for the windows throughout the house, wishing to produce a less formal atmosphere. The furniture was oak with flowered patterns, stripes and solid fabrics, a mishmash that somehow managed to be extremely attractive and welcoming. The mauve carpeting invited bare toes to sink into its plush depths.

It was just before noon on Thursday, and Margaret stood in front of the windows in the living room, watching for a glimpse of Amy's car.

Dressed in jeans and a pale green top, Margaret knew she appeared younger than forty-six. On more than one occasion she and Amy had been mistaken for sisters.

The two had the same slender figures, delicate features and big brown eyes. The major contrast was their hair; Margaret's was strawberry-blond, while Amy had inherited her dark curls from her father.

Margaret drew a steadying breath, then wrapped her hands around her elbows, hugging herself. She was admittedly nervous, a fact that did *not* please her one iota.

She was waiting for her own daughter, for heaven's sake, a woman who also had the title of being one of Margaret's very best friends. She not only loved Amy, she *liked* her as a person, and respected her beyond measure.

This, however, was a special occasion. Just as Amy had wanted Margaret's blessing of her intention to marry Blue Bishop, Margaret now hoped for acceptance of her announcement, the secret—the dream—that was actually coming true.

What she was going to reveal to Amy would be a tremendous surprise, Margaret knew. As close as she was to her daughter, as well as she understood her child, she had no idea how Amy would react to the news.

Margaret hoped—prayed—that a smile, not a

frown, would appear on Amy's face. But if Amy voiced a negative opinion, Margaret was prepared to continue on her chosen course. It would be up to Amy to adjust her attitude. Margaret would *not* reverse her etched-in-stone decision for anyone.

But as deeply as she believed in the rightness of what she was doing, something within her wished to have the support of the most important person in her life.

There were many who would shake their heads in total bewilderment as Margaret's plans unfolded, others who might very well be envious, and some who would strongly disapprove.

An image of Gibson McKinley flashed suddenly in Margaret's mind, and she frowned slightly as she realized it was there. Gib. She was looking forward to their dinner date Saturday night, had even considered buying a new dress for the outing.

She'd best enjoy being wined and dined by him, Margaret thought dryly. She was quite certain that if she chose to reveal her plans for the future while she was with Gib on Saturday, it would be the last she would see of the man.

Gib. Oh, yes, he was handsome and charming. The sensual impact he'd had on her had been startling, unsettling, yet exciting.

He'd awakened her sensuality from a slumber induced by her husband's death. Well, her womanly desires might as well go back to sleep, because she couldn't fathom Gib—or any man, for that matter—wanting anything to do with her dream.

"Amy," Margaret whispered as a familiar car turned into the driveway.

A soft smile of pride touched Margaret's lips as she watched her lovely daughter cross the lawn. Amy was wearing white shorts and a red, white and blue knit top. She looked happy and healthy, and so beautiful.

Amy entered the house and Margaret turned from the window.

"Mom?" Amy called.

"In here, sweetheart."

Amy came into the living room, and they met halfway to engage in a heartfelt hug.

"You look wonderful," Margaret said when they stepped apart. "Every time I see you you're more tanned. It's very becoming."

Amy laughed. "I've been outside a lot, because Blue is teaching me to ride a horse. I'm waiting for him to throw up his hands in defeat. I'm a disaster. I can't help myself, Mother. When I nudge the horse to go, I say 'please?' Blue has a fit, because I'm supposed to let that poor beast know I'm in charge. A wimpy little 'please?' doesn't cut it, says the master of the Rocking B ranch. The whole thing is a hoot."

Margaret's laughter mingled with Amy's as they walked through the house to the eating area at the end of the sunny kitchen. It had a bay window with padded cushions covered in material that was a splash of vibrant wildflowers. Two chairs with flowered seats edged the glass-top table that was set for two, with linen napkins that matched the window-seat cushions.

Over the years the Madison family had used the cheerful nook for their meals, reserving the formal dining room for special occasions.

"Aha" Amy said, pointing one finger in the air as she looked at the table. "The plate. I had a feeling this was more than just a casual invitation. My goodness, that plate could tell some stories, couldn't it? The question for today is, who is using it?"

The plate that was presently the center of attention was made of stoneware glazed in bright red. In white letters around the rim were the words "This is your special day."

"Well," Margaret began, "you know the tradition of the plate. The birthday person, of course, will have their dinner served on it.

"It's also used for momentous occasions, such as good report cards, and the day you got the cast off your arm after you broke it falling out of the mulberry tree in the backyard.

"Your father had the honor of its use when he made a hole in one on the golf course. The list just goes on and on."

"So many memories are connected to that plate," Amy said softly.

"Yes."

"So," Amy said, looking at her mother, "I haven't done anything to deserve having my lunch on the plate. That means you must have an announcement to make. The plate is yours today."

Margaret nodded. "The plate is mine. Sit down, sweetheart. I made a big fruit salad, which is one of your favorite summer meals, along with crunchy French bread and iced tea."

"I'll help you carry the goodies to the table, Mom."

"No, no, I'm fine."

Amy slid onto a cushioned seat, glanced at the shiny red plate, then studied her mother as Margaret busied herself bringing the food to the table.

What was going on? Amy wondered. Her mother seemed a bit tense, but not upset or worried. No, it was...bubbling excitement, anticipation of some kind, that was emanating from Margaret Madison. Whatever was on her mom's agenda was important enough to deserve using the red plate.

"Mother," Amy said, "I can't stand it. Tell me what's behind this invitation to lunch, and the using of the special plate, before I jump out of my shoes."

Margaret poured iced tea into the glasses, set the pitcher on the table, then sat down in a chair opposite Amy. After spreading the napkin on her lap, Margaret met her daughter's attentive gaze.

"Serve yourself some salad, Amy."

"Lunch can wait. What is your news?"

Margaret shifted her eyes to the plate, then slowly traced the white letters with one fingertip, remembering some of the events the plate had witnessed. She drew a steadying breath, then looked at Amy again.

"Amy, I pride myself on the way I've accepted

the major changes in my life. You went off to college, which created a void in this house, then your father died so suddenly. There have been some dark, cloudy days in the past.''

Amy nodded, her eyes riveted on her mother's face.

''In the five years since your father died, I've kept busy, as you know. I'm very grateful for the way he provided for me financially.

''I spend many hours a week giving piano lessons to underprivileged children. I've been on various community committees, headed up fund-raisers for charities.

''During those years you popped in and out of here on a regular basis, sometimes spending the night in your old room.''

''Yes,'' Amy said, unsure what her mother was getting at, ''that's true.''

''As we were making plans for your wedding,'' Margaret went on, ''it really began to sink in that I was about to experience another big change in my life. You would have your own home, and a husband. My nest, I realized, would be truly empty when you became Amy Madison Bishop.''

''Oh, but—''

''I know what you're going to say, Amy. You'll visit as often as you can, but you're a married woman now, who also has a career. I'm not complaining, or feeling sorry for myself. I'm simply acknowledging another milestone in my life. It's up to me to fill whatever empty space has been created from it.''

"Yes, I see," Amy said, nodding slowly. "That makes sense, I guess."

"What shall I do, I asked myself. Travel? Take classes at the university? Devote even more time to giving piano lessons? I'm not without many options.

"Then I asked myself what had brought me the greatest joy and sense of fulfillment through the years. Being a wife and mother. Those roles enhanced the essence of who I am."

Amy's eyes widened and she stiffened. "Oh, my gosh, you're getting married. You're getting married? To whom? I had no idea there was someone serious in your life. You're getting married?"

Margaret smiled. "No, Amy, I am *not* getting married."

"But you said that the two roles that had brought you the greatest joy—"

"You picked the wrong one," Margaret said.

"Pardon me?"

Margaret reached over and covered Amy's hand with one of hers.

"My darling daughter," she said, "I'm going to adopt a baby. I'm going to raise one more baby girl, who will be your little sister."

Amy opened her mouth, shut it, then tried again. When she spoke, her voice was hardly more than a squeak.

"You're adopting a baby?" she said, then shook her head and laughed. "Oh, you are not." She frowned and leaned toward her mother. "Are you?"

Margaret smiled. It was a soft smile, a womanly, motherly, peaceful smile.

"Yes, I really am. She's adorable, Amy. I'm so eager for you to meet her. She's fourteen months old and—"

"Wait, wait," Amy said, waving her hands in the air. "You're going too fast for me. Mom, please, start at the beginning. I'm so stunned and I need to digest all this. Take it slow and easy for my befuddled brain."

"Let's have some lunch while we talk," Margaret said, spooning fruit salad onto her plate.

"I can't eat," Amy said, pressing one hand to her stomach. "My tummy is jumpy."

Margaret laughed. "You started using that description when you were about six years old. You simply couldn't go to the first day of school, or the doctor, or the dentist, because your tummy was jumpy. Eat your lunch."

"Yes, ma'am."

They ate in silence for several minutes.

"Mother," Amy said finally, "speak to me."

"Well, I've told you a great deal already, sweetheart. I went through another major change in my life during the weeks we were planning your wedding.

"I knew then what I wanted to do, what my most secret and deepest desire was. Admittedly, I couldn't imagine that it would be possible to adopt a baby at my age and with my single status."

"But it *is* possible?"

"Indeed it is," Margaret said, nodding. "If a person isn't allergic to mountains of paperwork. I had to get a complete physical, provide names of those who would write letters of recommendation for me, produce a financial statement, income tax returns—oh, my, it did seem endless."

"Why didn't you tell me that all this was going on? You could have shared it with me, Mother, from the very beginning."

"I'm sorry if your feelings are hurt because I didn't, Amy. One reason was because the spotlight was on you and your pending marriage to Blue, which was as it should be. Then you were newly married and it didn't seem the right time."

"Yes, but—" Amy said.

"The other thing was that I was emotionally shaky myself. I was assigned a caseworker, who interviewed me here, looking over my home in the process. I was attempting to keep a part of me in emotional reserve in the event that something went wrong and my application wasn't approved. Please understand, Amy. I needed to do this alone, keep it private."

"But you *were* approved?"

Margaret smiled. "Yes. My paperwork is presently on a judge's desk somewhere in the bureaucratic jungle in downtown Houston. I'm waiting for my official certification papers to be signed. They never know how long that will take. It often depends on which judge received the file."

"I see. All right, you'll become certified. Is that the proper term? Then what?"

"Well, during this waiting period, my caseworker processed the paperwork for a toddler in foster care. The birth mother finally decided she would put the baby up for adoption."

"Why?"

"She's seventeen years old. She'd decided to keep her baby, but it was so difficult for her. She released the infant to foster care temporarily six months ago, but..."

"But?" Amy said.

"She didn't visit the baby during those months. Not once. She returned to the world of parties and fast living. Her parents had disowned her when she became pregnant. A few weeks ago she showed up with signed documents from her and the birth father, relinquishing the baby for adoption. They were off to California and what they believed would be exciting adventures."

"Incredible," Amy said.

"My caseworker asked me if I would like to go with her to the foster home and meet the baby. I did and, oh, my, it was love at first sight. I'm welcome there as often as I want to come. I've fed the baby, played with her, given her a bath, rocked her to sleep at night. She smiles when she sees me now, toddles right over to me and raises her little arms for me to pick her up.

"The moment my certification comes through, I'll bring her home. The official application for adoption will be filed, and down the road we appear before a judge for the final decree. But even now, in my heart, she's mine.''

"What's...her name?"

"Her birth mother named her Moonbeam."

"You're kidding."

"I'm afraid not. There will be a new birth certificate issued, showing me as her mother. It will also have her new name...Alison Margaret Madison.''

"Alison," Amy said quietly.

"The foster mother where Alison is staying has been wonderful about allowing me to visit, and she has been calling her Alison, too. I've fixed up the spare bedroom as a nursery. Would you like to see it?''

"No," Amy said. "I mean...yes, of course I would. I..." She shook her head, then got to her feet, turning her back to Margaret.

"Amy?" Margaret said anxiously.

Amy spun around, her eyes filled with tears.

"I can't believe how I feel," she said. "What a horrible person I am. Terrible thoughts are rushing through my mind, hammering at me.''

"Tell me. Go ahead, sweetheart, say what you're feeling.''

"*I'm* your baby," Amy said, flinging out her arms. "Why are you replacing me? Oh, God, that is so unfair, so childish and selfish. I'm married to Blue and hope to have his babies. I'm living the life I want, the one I've chosen. You have every right to do that, too. What's wrong with me? I'm jealous of a little baby. But you're *my* mother. *Mine.*"

Margaret rose and went to Amy, encircling her with her arms.

"I've done a lot of reading in the past weeks regarding adoption, and what you're feeling is perfectly normal, no matter how old you are."

"What I'm doing, the way I'm acting, is disgusting," Amy said, sniffling.

"No, no, it's not. It's dear, very sweet, very loving. And, Amy? You'll always be my baby. Nothing will change that. Even when you become a mother yourself, you'll still be my baby."

Amy returned her mother's hug. "I love you, Mom. I respect and admire you more than I can begin to tell you. Alison is a lucky little girl."

"*I'm* the one who feels blessed."

Amy moved back so she could look directly into her mother's eyes. "I'm ready for a tour of the nursery."

"Wonderful," Margaret said, smiling. "Thank you, darling. I know this was quite a shock."

"Well, one thing is for sure," Amy said, as they left the kitchen.

"Which is?"

"I'd better get the hang of riding a horse. It's going to be very embarrassing if my little sister is galloping across the fields with Blue, while I'm still in the corral begging my horse to *please* move."

Margaret's and Amy's laughter danced through the air, seeming to fill the large house to overflowing.

* * *

That night Margaret tossed and turned, unable to sleep. She finally left her bed and went into the kitchen, where she made herself a mug of warm milk. As she sipped the soothing drink, she wandered aimlessly around the living room, replaying over and over in her mind the scene that had taken place with Amy.

She was not, she knew, having difficulty sleeping because she was distressed about Amy's reaction to the news about Alison.

No, the heart-to-heart with Amy had been so precious, so endearing, it was as though her mind were insisting on holding fast to it in vivid detail, not wishing for it to become just a memory.

Margaret snapped off the lamp on the end table and went down the hall to the room she'd prepared for Alison. She turned on the night-light, casting a soft glow in the room. Standing statue still, the mug of milk cradled in her hands, she swept her gaze over the nursery.

She had decorated it in bright, happy colors. The crib, dresser and changing table were white, and the paper on one wall boasted prancing clowns. A bouquet of felt balloons hung on the wall next to the crib. There was a toy box containing a variety of treasures, and the dresser drawers held clothes ready to be worn.

Margaret crossed the room and sat down in a rocking chair.

Jack had bought her this chair when she'd discovered she was pregnant with Amy. She'd spent many hours rocking her precious daughter in the lovely piece of furniture.

Now she would rock another daughter while sitting in that chair. But this time there would be no Jack waiting for her after she'd settled their baby for the night.

Margaret sipped the cooling milk, then nodded.

She was alone. She would raise Alison alone and they'd do just fine; they'd make a terrific team. She'd thoroughly examined the issues of being a single, older mom, and she was at peace with all the avenues she'd covered in her mind.

"Soon, Alison," Margaret whispered. "Very soon now, you'll be coming home."

She rocked back and forth slowly, allowing the contentment she was feeling to consume her, wrap itself around her like a comforting cloak.

When she finally returned to bed, Margaret fell asleep immediately.

But when she awoke the next morning, she realized she'd dreamed about Gibson McKinley. She'd been holding out a bundle wrapped in a pink blanket, urging him to take it into his arms. Gib had shaken his head and turned away, disappearing into a heavy, gray fog.

And in the dream Margaret had buried her face in the pink blanket and wept.

Chapter Three

By Saturday evening Margaret had managed to erase the memory of the disturbing dream about Gib and the baby from her mind.

She'd had a lovely day, she thought as she floated a kelly green silk dress over her head. She'd spent the morning with Alison, thoroughly enjoying every minute shared with the baby.

Then she'd shopped, eventually finding the pretty green dress. The beauty parlor had been her next stop, where she'd had her hair shampooed and trimmed.

After a long, leisurely soak in a lilac-scented bubble bath, she'd begun to prepare for her evening out with Gib.

Margaret fastened her two-inch strappy sandals,

then scrutinized her reflection in the floor-length mirror that hung on the back of her bedroom door.

Not bad, she decided. She could hold her own among the forty-something crowd. The softly draped neckline of the dress was flattering, the color perfect for her hair and complexion, the midcalf length of the swirling skirt just right.

"Well, aren't you full of yourself, Mrs. Madison?" she said with a burst of laughter.

Still smiling, she slipped the few items she wanted from her purse into a small clutch bag, then left the bedroom.

In the living room she set the evening bag on an end table, fluffed several throw pillows on the sofa, then sat down in an easy chair. In the next moment she was up again and wandering around the large room.

Her days of leisurely bubble baths were numbered, she realized. Mothers with toddlers were known for taking baths and showers with record-breaking speed. There would also be no more spur-of-the-moment shopping sprees to take advantage of sales. Her schedule would revolve around Alison's.

The community center where she gave free piano lessons was attempting to find volunteers to take Margaret's place already. She'd promised to return on a limited basis once she and Alison were in a comfortable routine.

But for the first weeks—even months, if necessary—after she brought Alison home, Margaret's attention would be focused entirely on her new daughter.

Any day now, Margaret mused as she walked through the room, the telephone would ring and she'd hear the social worker announce the arrival of the signed certification papers. On that glorious day she'd unpack the car seat waiting in its box in the garage, secure it in the back seat and drive across town to pick up Alison and bring her home.

Home, Margaret thought, stopping to look around the living room. How wonderful it would be to once again hear the music of a child's laughter in the house. There would be toys scattered everywhere, tiny fingerprints on the furniture, spills of juice and crumbs from crackers on the kitchen floor.

The big, quiet house with everything spotless would be in a shambles, the silence broken by baby squeals and giggles, and crying that would bring Margaret instantly to her feet.

The knickknacks on the end tables would have to be removed, along with the flowers and magazines on the coffee table. She'd already had a handyman install safety latches on every drawer and cupboard in the house.

A tiny miracle, weighing less than twenty-five pounds and standing only about thirty inches tall, was going to turn her home and life upside down. And Margaret could hardly wait.

No more leisurely bubble baths, she mentally repeated. And after that magical telephone call there would be no more Gibson McKinley. So be it.

Margaret turned as she heard a car door slam, announcing Gib's arrival.

She was determined to have a fabulous time tonight. It would be her last hurrah before once again embracing the world of diapers, teething and sticky little fingers. A world she did not expect any man in her age bracket to want any part of.

Margaret smoothed the skirt of her dress, lifted her chin and smiled as she waited for the doorbell to ring.

Gib swept his gaze over the yard and house as he approached the front door.

Very nice, he thought. The ranch-style home was attractive, and probably more practical than his own two-story house. The day would come when he'd have to sell the house and move, when he was too old to manage the stairs.

Lord, McKinley, knock it off. He was turning fifty this year, not a hundred and fifty.

Fifty. He would have been on this earth for a half century, which was a hell of a lot of years. Oh, for Pete's sake, forget it, he told himself.

What he should concentrate on was the lovely lady waiting for him beyond that front door. He'd thought of Margaret often since their lunch together, and he was looking forward to the evening ahead.

That Margaret Madison had never been far from his mind since their lunch together was due, of course, to his neglecting his social life over the past weeks. It certainly wasn't Margaret herself who had

had a profound effect on him. It was the fact that she happened to be a beautiful, intelligent woman.

He liked women, respected and admired them. He enjoyed talking with them, hearing a woman's logic. The majority of women he knew had an intriguing way of approaching life, bringing depth and emotion to even the simplest situation.

He had no intention of ever marrying again, but women were, without a doubt, major players in his existence. And yes, indeed, Gib thought as he pressed the doorbell, he was *definitely* looking forward to the hours he was about to spend with Margaret.

The front door opened, pulling Gib from his thoughts.

"Hello, Gib," Margaret said, smiling. She stepped back, allowing room for him to enter. "Come in."

Gib matched her smile as he came into the house.

"Good evening, Margaret," he said. She really was beautiful. Absolutely lovely. That aura of class was present again, too. "It's very nice to see you."

Margaret shut the door, then turned to look at Gib. "Would you care for a drink before we go?" she said. Heavens, he was handsome. The dark suit with the pale blue shirt and dark tie did wonderful things for his thick black hair and tanned skin. The streaks of gray at his temples were so perfect, it appeared as though they'd been painted distinguishingly in place. "And it's nice to see you again, too."

"I've made a reservation," Gib said, "and the traffic seems even heavier than usual tonight. I think we'd better be on our way." He looked around the large living room. "You have a very attractive home. I like it."

"Thank you. I've lived here many years and I still get a feeling of peace whenever I walk through the door. This home has always seemed to wrap itself around me like a snuggly blanket."

Oh, yes, Gib reaffirmed in his mind, he enjoyed the way certain women's minds worked and the charm with which they expressed themselves. In that category, Margaret Madison had just gone to the top of the list.

Margaret snapped on a lamp, picked up her clutch purse, then they left the house. Gib assisted her into a plush, late-model silver sedan that smelled deliciously of new leather.

As Gib drove out of the subdivision and into the surging traffic, he glanced over at Margaret, then redirected his attention to the road.

"I take it from what you said that you didn't even consider moving to a smaller house, or perhaps a condo, after your husband passed away."

"No, not for a second," Margaret said. "I don't feel as though I'm rattling around with more space than I need." And she'd be even more appreciative of the size of the house when Alison came home. "And you? Did you move to a condo once you found yourself alone?"

Gib shook his head. "No, I stayed put." Despite the fact that there were more bad memories than good within those walls, he thought ruefully. "I have a two-story and I go weeks at a stretch not even stepping into some of the rooms." He laughed. "On the way to pick you up, I was thinking that I would have to sell the place when I'm too old to manage the stairs."

"For heaven's sake," Margaret said, looking over at him. "You actually spent time thinking about such a thing? That is years and years in the future, Gib."

He shrugged. "I suppose, but it did hit me that when I celebrate my fiftieth birthday this year, I will have been on this earth for a half century. That's a rather overwhelming thought."

"Gibson McKinley," Margaret said, laughing, "are you planning on having a midlife crisis?"

"Lord, I hope not," he said, smiling. "I'd have to go out and buy a red sports car, get some gold chains to wear around my neck and find a buxom blonde half my age to dangle on my arm. I'm much too busy at work to take all that on. It would never fit into my schedule."

Margaret's smile faded slowly. "But you *are* a bit concerned about turning fifty, aren't you?"

"I didn't think I was, but it *has* popped into my mind with regularity lately. I feel as though…oh, I don't know…as though I should be stopping and taking inventory at such a momentous milestone, making certain I'm where I really wish to be in my life."

"That has merit," Margaret said, nodding. "I did that recently myself, when I realized that Amy was going to have her own home, a husband and a career to focus on. I got in touch with myself and...well, like you said...took inventory.''

''And? What did you discover?''

Oh, dear, Margaret thought, this conversation had somehow headed in the last direction she would have wished for it to go. This was neither the time nor the place to blurt out the fact that she was in the process of adopting a baby.

She wasn't that certain she would *ever* share her cherished news with Gibson. He might not call her again after this outing, depending on how their evening together went. If she never heard from him again, there was no need for him to know about Alison.

She was hiding her plans, holding them close to her heart, being very selective about who knew about them until Alison was actually at home, where she belonged.

''Margaret?''

''Oh, I... Gib, would you mind turning the air-conditioning down a little bit?''

''Sure thing,'' he said, flicking a dial on the dashboard. ''How's that?''

''Much better. Thank you. Oh, look at the gorgeous flowers in that park over there. Aren't they lovely?''

''Mmm,'' he said absently.

He hadn't been mistaken the day he'd had lunch with Margaret, Gib thought. Nor had his journalistic instincts been working overtime without just cause. Margaret Madison *did* have a secret of some sort.

She'd just skittered skillfully away from answering the question about what she'd discovered during the personal inventory she'd conducted.

Interesting. Intriguing. And, oh, yes, he most definitely wanted to know what was going on in this fascinating woman's mind *and* in her life. Was she putting a major change into operation after her inner inventory?

Stay alert, McKinley, he told himself. He'd listen for clues, as well as watch and wait for an opportunity to broach the subject again.

The restaurant Gib had chosen was one of Houston's finest. It was large, but due to the clever design of its three tiers, the diners were still afforded a sense of intimacy. State-of-the-art acoustics, as well as plush carpeting, kept the noise level to a minimum. The food was excellent and the service top-notch.

Margaret and Gib chatted while they waited for the shrimp scampi with steak dinners they'd ordered. Conversation flowed easily from one topic to the next, and they were soon sampling the cuisine.

"Delicious," Margaret said.

"I'm glad you're enjoying it," Gib said.

"I've never been to this restaurant before. It's very elegant." Margaret laughed softly. "I'm certainly not envious of the person who has to dust all those chandeliers."

"There are even more to keep clean in the ballroom. Would you like to dance after we eat? They have a very good combo that plays a little bit of everything.''

"Yes, that sounds very delightful," Margaret said, smiling.

Dancing with Gib, she thought. They had danced the night away on the evening they'd first met. Oh, yes, she most definitely would like to be held in Gibson's strong arms again, to sway to the music, to be lost in a wondrous, sensuously misty world made up of only the two of them.

She would once again have a Cinderella night with her very own Prince Charming. The difference between herself and fairy-tale Cindy was that the prince would not be showing up at Margaret's door once he learned her secret.

No, Gibson McKinley wouldn't elect to keep company with a woman who had to hire a baby-sitter before she could venture out on a date. Gib had finished his stint of diapers and chicken pox years before with his daughter, Betsy. While he said he thoroughly enjoyed his grandchildren, he had made it clear that he was happy to send them home after a visit.

So this night, Margaret mused, was her grand finale. She was fortunate to have been granted one before she became a housebound mommy. She'd go out with a bang, savoring every moment, every memory made, with Gib.

Margaret looked at Gib from beneath her lashes, watching him eat his dinner, and she welcomed the stirring of desire that she felt low and deep within her body.

She was in a strange mood, she realized, a rather reckless, no-rules-apply frame of mind. Oh, yes, this was definitely *her* night and, as the saying went, she was going to go for the gusto.

Margaret and Gib both declined the offer of dessert and finished the meal with coffee and a rich, smooth brandy served in paper-thin snifters. The warmth from the brandy met and mingled with the heat of desire thrumming through Margaret, fanning it into licking flames she made no effort to quell.

Gib raised his snifter in a toast. "To a lovely evening and an even lovelier lady."

"Thank you, sir," Margaret said, touching her glass to his.

She took another sip of the brandy, then set the snifter on the table, cradling it gently between her hands.

"You intrigue me, Margaret Madison," Gib said, looking directly into her brown eyes.

"I do?" she said, smiling. "Intrigue. That hints of the mysterious. I consider myself an open, what-you-see-is-what-you-get type of woman." Well, that was how she usually perceived herself. She *did* have a secret at the moment, but since Gib had no clue about that, his overall conception of her was wrong. "You need to choose a word other than intrigue."

"No, that's the one I want," Gib said, smiling. "Yes, you're open, honest and real, and don't play the games often carried out in the singles scene. You're beautiful, intelligent, classy, talented—"

"Please," Margaret said, laughing. "Enough. You'll turn my head, Mr. McKinley."

"And," he went on, "you're intriguing. There's a mysterious aura about you, a sense of secrecy. I do believe, Ms. Madison, that there is something of importance that you're not sharing with me. Do you care to comment on that?"

Margaret's eyes widened in shock for a moment, then she averted her gaze from Gib's as she felt a warm flush stain her cheeks.

Dear heaven, she thought, was Gibson McKinley a mind reader?

Did he have psychic powers of some sort like Amy's brother-in-law, Tux Bishop?

Or were his journalistic instincts combining with her lack of experience at harboring a secret?

Whichever was the case, she had no intention of pouring out her heart about Alison in the middle of a crowded restaurant.

"Margaret?"

"What? Oh, no, I have no comment to make." She managed to produce a small smile. "You're being fanciful. You're not at *The Holler* this evening, Gib. You can turn off your reporter's radar."

Gib chuckled and shook his head. "All right, Margaret, we'll go with that...for now. However, I still believe... Well, enough said at the moment. Are you ready to go into the ballroom?"

"Yes," she said. More than ready. She wanted to

leave the table, the probing questions and the penetrating scrutiny coming from Gib's dark, compelling, *knowing* eyes. "I'd like to stop at the powder room first, though."

"That's fine. You go ahead, while I settle the check. I'll meet you in the reception area."

Margaret nodded, picked up her purse and got to her feet. Gib watched her make her way across the crowded room and down the stairways to the main level.

Lovely, he thought again. Margaret moved with a natural grace that was extremely appealing. He'd seen the men she passed giving her second looks, appreciative glances, and he had registered a sense of possessiveness, pride and—yes, all right, he'd admit it—a flash of jealousy that was very uncharacteristic for him.

Gib caught the eye of the waiter and signaled for the check.

Of course, he hadn't been behaving true to form in regard to Margaret from the first time he'd met her. He was *not* accustomed to having a woman consume his thoughts.

His adolescent hovering over the telephone, trying to reach Margaret after Amy and Blue's wedding, was something he'd like to erase from his memory bank.

The high level of anticipation of this evening with Margaret was also bordering on the ridiculous.

Oh, she was a spell weaver, all right, the lovely Margaret. And she *was* intriguing. And she *did* have a secret, no matter how much she attempted to deny it.

Gib took his wallet from his pocket and slipped a credit card free, tapping it on the table as he narrowed his eyes.

Enough cloak-and-dagger for one night, McKinley, he told himself. In a handful of minutes he'd be taking Margaret into his arms on the dance floor, feeling her slender, feminine body pressed to his, inhaling her delicate aroma of spring flowers.

That was what he was going to concentrate on for the remainder of the evening.

The ballroom had been given the same attention to detail as the dining room. The multitude of chandeliers had been dimmed to create a romantic glow over the large expanse.

A carpeted area dotted with small, round tables and upholstered chairs surrounded the gleaming wood floor, and tiny, shaded lamps shone on the center of each table.

Margaret set her clutch purse on one of the tables as Gib flipped a square card over to read Reserved. The band began playing a dreamy waltz as Gib escorted Margaret to the dance floor.

Gib turned to Margaret with his arms extended slightly toward her. Their eyes met. Time stopped. Hearts skipped a beat.

Feeling as though they were moving in tantalizingly slow motion, they anticipated the moment of the embrace yet to come. Memories from the wedding reception and the hours spent in each other's arms teased with rich, vivid pictures.

Slowly. Waiting. Arms reaching, barely touching. Desire beginning to soar.

Then Margaret was in Gib's arms and he took a sharp breath, realizing only then that he hadn't been breathing. He nestled Margaret close to his heated body and began to waltz.

As Margaret was enveloped in the strength and blatant masculinity of Gibson, she sighed. It was a soft sigh, a womanly sound of pure feminine pleasure. She felt delicate, fragile, beautiful and safe.

For the remaining hours of this magical Cinderella night, she didn't have to do anything except simply *be*, Margaret thought dreamily.

She wasn't strong, independent, organized Margaret.

She wasn't a woman alone about to take on the challenge of raising a child from a baby to an emotionally and physically healthy adult.

She wasn't levelheaded Margaret Madison, who thought carefully before making major decisions, weighed and measured, sifted and sorted, leaving no detail unaddressed.

She was just a woman, rejoicing in her own femininity, welcoming the heated desire thrumming through her.

She was being held in the protective embrace of a desirable man, gliding gracefully over the dance floor as though she were a gossamer butterfly.

They danced. One lilting melody followed another. They didn't talk or think, they simply danced, savoring the feel and aroma of each other.

The people around them disappeared beyond the sensual mist that encased them. Passion burned brighter, hotter, creating such incredible heat. There was only the two of them, and want, need and beautiful music.

"Margaret," Gib finally said, his voice hoarse.

That was all he said, only her name, in a tone that spoke volumes. Margaret understood the message, the question not asked, and knew the answer without hesitation.

"Yes," she whispered.

Staying close, arms entwined, they left the dance floor, the ballroom, then the building. The drive to Margaret's was a blur as she rested her head on Gib's shoulder.

At Margaret's house they went into the bedroom. They shed their clothes in the soft glow of the lamp on the nightstand, stood naked before each other, gloried in what they saw.

"You're so exquisite," Gib said, placing one hand on Margaret's cheek.

She turned her head to kiss his palm, then met his gaze again.

"So are you," she said.

Cool, pastel sheets received their heated bodies as they moved onto the bed, reaching instantly for each other, eagerly, urgently.

They kissed, caressed, tasted, explored, marveling in all they discovered.

Gib drew the sweet bounty of one of Margaret's breasts into his mouth, stroking the nipple to a taut bud with his tongue. She closed her eyes as she sank her fingers into his thick hair, urging him closer yet, offering more.

He paid homage to her other breast, then slid downward, trailing a ribbon of kisses along her flat stomach, then lower yet.

"Oh, Gib," Margaret said, her voice a near sob. "Please. I want you so much. Now, Gib. Please."

He surged upward to capture her lips in a searing kiss, his tongue plummeting deep into her mouth.

Then he entered her, thrusting into her moist heat, the dark haven of her femininity. He brought to her all that he was as a man, and she received him, welcomed him, with all that she was as a woman.

They were one.

And the beautiful music played on as they danced.

The tempo increased and they met it in perfect synchronization—partners, equal, giving, taking, in harmony.

The crescendo was magnificent. The music was resounding; cymbals crashed, trumpets blared, violins sang like a chorus of angels.

The final note held them immobile for countless moments, before releasing them to drift down, down, slowly and reverently.

"Gib," Margaret whispered.

That was all she said, only his name, but he knew.

Their lovemaking had been wondrous, beyond the scope of past experiences, or future imagination.

With heads resting on the same pillow, they slept, sated, contented…and awed.

Chapter Four

As the fingers of dawn's light tiptoed across the bed, Gib stirred and opened his eyes, his mental alarm clock never allowing him the luxury of sleeping late.

He turned his head, a quiet smile forming on his lips as he looked at Margaret sleeping peacefully beside him.

She was on her stomach facing him, one hand beneath the pillow, the other splayed on the sheet in his direction. Her short, strawberry-blond hair was in fetching disarray, and her lips were parted slightly, hinting at the sweet darkness within.

Heated desire began to coil low in Gib's body, and he pulled his gaze from Margaret to frown at the ceiling.

Lord, he thought, he couldn't even glance at Margaret Madison without wanting her. He'd awakened in the night, reaching for her, and she'd come to him, willingly, eagerly. It was as though he couldn't get enough of her, had fallen under a magical spell she'd cast over him.

That behavior, Gibson, as his grandmother used to say, *will never do.*

Gib chuckled softly.

He'd worry later about the strong attraction he had for Margaret, deal with it, get it under his control. Right now he was a very sexually satisfied man, who was feeling terrific.

A lazy, no-stress Sunday stretched before him, and he sincerely hoped Margaret would agree to spend the day with him.

What he would do, he decided, was invade Margaret's kitchen and make a pot of coffee. He'd bring her a steaming cup of morning brew, wake her with a kiss, then suggest they make plans for the day.

With a nod of satisfaction, Gib moved off the bed with an economy of motion so as not to wake Margaret. He pulled on his shorts and trousers, then left the bedroom.

As he walked down the hallway, his attention was drawn to a splash of rainbow colors on the carpeting ahead of him. He stopped in front of the rainbow, then saw that a door to his right was slightly ajar, color escaping from the narrow opening.

He hesitated a moment over the propriety of peering uninvited into one of the rooms in Margaret's home, but his curiosity about the source of the vibrant rainbow got the better of him. He flattened his hand on the door and opened it slowly.

He stiffened, a heavy frown of confusion knitting his brows.

A baby nursery? Yes, that was what this was, a fully equipped room for a baby. The rainbow had been created by the morning sun inching through the slats on one of the shutters that wasn't tightly closed on the window. The sun had found a multicolored sun-catcher in the shape of a clown, which was suspended from the ceiling.

Gib went into the room, his eyes darting around, cataloging all that he saw.

Why on earth did Margaret Madison have a picture-perfect nursery set up in her house? Surely it wasn't left over from Amy's baby days. No, that was ridiculous. Amy had left home as a young woman. Margaret wasn't a neurotic nut who had left the baby's nursery intact and moved her daughter to another room. Forget that.

Had there been another infant? One who had died? Was this a shrine of some sort? No. Again that didn't fit the Margaret he knew. Besides, there was a crisp newness to everything in the room.

Was Amy pregnant with Blue's baby? Had excited grandmother-to-be Margaret jumped the gun and prepared a place for the baby to visit months in advance of its actual arrival?

That had possibilities, Gib decided. In fact, that

was the only reasonable explanation for what he'd discovered.

He ran one hand over his beard-roughened chin and narrowed his eyes.

Bingo, he thought. He *knew* that Margaret had a secret. He'd just pieced together the mysterious puzzle.

Amy Madison Bishop was pregnant. She didn't want it widely known until she was further along, and had sworn her mother to secrecy. Excited beyond belief, Margaret had gone ahead and furnished a complete nursery for her first grandchild.

Gib smiled and shook his head as he left the room, pulling the door closed to exactly where he had originally found it.

Once an investigative reporter, always an investigative reporter, he thought smugly, resuming his trek to the kitchen. He'd stayed alert, gathered evidence and solved the mystery of Margaret's secret.

Man, he was good. He still had the knack for digging out a story when he set his mind to it. The old instincts were as razor sharp as they'd always been.

Humming off tune and feeling extremely pleased with himself, Gib found the makings for coffee, then waited for it to brew, admiring the large, attractive kitchen and eating nook in the process.

With a mug of hot coffee in each hand, he returned to the master bedroom. Margaret hadn't stirred from where he'd left her. He set one mug on the nightstand, sat down next to Margaret on the bed, then leaned over to gently kiss her soft cheek.

"Margaret?" he said quietly. "I come bearing gifts. Well, one gift. A hot cup of coffee."

"Hmm?" she said, not opening her eyes.

"Coffee, my lady, hand delivered to you in the comfort of your own bed."

Margaret rolled over, opening her eyes at the same time. She blinked once, again, frowned, then finally smiled.

"Good morning, Gib," she said. "Coffee?"

"Yes, ma'am."

Gib stood so Margaret could scoot upward. She shoved the pillow against the headboard and tucked the sheet under her arms to cover her naked breasts.

"I hope you don't mind my waking you." Gib sat back down, then handed Margaret the mug.

Margaret shook her head, then took a sip of the hot drink.

"Mmm," she said. "Perfect. This is a nice treat...coffee in bed. Thank you, Gib."

"My pleasure." He picked up the other mug and raised it in a toast. "My sincere congratulations, Margaret. I toast you and the new role you'll be enjoying in your life. I also toast me for having figured out your *intriguing* secret. I *knew* you were holding something back from me. Well, your secret is safe with me for as long as instructed."

Margaret frowned as a knot tightened in her stomach. She looked at Gib intently, noted his smile, the mischief dancing in his dark eyes, heard the chipper, albeit smug, tone of his voice.

"What are you talking about?" she said.

"Your secret. I discovered what it is."

"Oh?" she said, hardly breathing.

"I was walking toward the kitchen to make the coffee and saw a rainbow in the hallway. Miss Manners wouldn't approve, I suppose, but I pushed open the door to the room where the rainbow was coming from. And? Bingo. I saw it...the baby nursery."

Margaret's eyes widened and a shiver coursed down her spine. She grasped the mug with both hands, holding it tightly.

"Don't look so stricken," Gib said, still smiling. "I won't let on I know when Amy comes to *The Holler* to turn in her stories. I'll act very surprised and pleased when she finally shares her news with me."

"Amy?"

Gib chuckled. "I've heard of excited grandparents-to-be, Margaret, but you win the prize. That snazzy nursery is prepared as though the baby is arriving tomorrow. And baby-safe latches already installed in the kitchen? You're really something. Actually, it's rather sweet. You will be, in my not-humble-at-all opinion, a fantastic grandmother."

Well, Margaret thought, this was it. She had to tell Gib about Alison before his misconceptions of what he'd found went any further. To keep silent longer would fall into the area of a lie of omission, and she did *not* lie, under any circumstances.

Margaret took a sip of coffee as she attempted to gather her thoughts. She slid a glance at Gib, who had tilted his head back to drain his mug, and her heart did a funny little two-step.

Magnificent, she mused. Gib looked so earthy, raw and real, with his tousled hair, the dark stubble of his beard, his bare, tanned chest beckoning to her fingertips to weave through the swirl of black curls.

Last night the lovemaking they'd shared had been exquisite, beautiful beyond description. She had *never* experienced such heights of passion.

It wasn't fair to Jack to compare their many years together with one night with Gibson McKinley, but she couldn't help it. Gib had taken her up to and beyond a level of sensuality she hadn't even known existed.

Back to reality, Margaret, she told herself. This was the morning after, the light of the new day. And because of what Gib had discovered in her home and the erroneous conclusions he'd drawn, it was truth time.

But the memories of her Cinderella night with Gibson were hers to keep, and she would...forever.

She set her mug on the nightstand and Gib slid his in place next to it.

"Gib," she said, folding her hands in her lap, "do you remember when we talked about taking a personal inventory of our lives?"

"Sure. You said you'd done exactly that when you realized that Amy was really leaving the nest to tend to her own. What you didn't tell me was what you found out about yourself."

"Yes, I know. I was...well, secretive about it."

"Little did you know that you were dealing with Sherlock Holmes here." Gib laughed. "You should have seen your face when I figured it out."

"But you were wrong."

Gib's smile changed instantly to a frown. "What do you mean?"

"Amy isn't pregnant. Well, if she is, she hasn't told me. The nursery you saw is...is for *my* baby."

Gib opened his mouth, shut it, then tried again. "What?"

"I discovered that my greatest joys in life had come from being a wife and mother. I'm no longer a wife, nor do I intend to be again. My daughter is grown, married, focusing on her husband, home and career. I'm not needed by Amy day in, day out any longer."

"Go on," Gib said, looking at her intently.

"While I have no desire to be a wife again, I *could* be a full-time mother." Margaret paused and took a steadying breath. "Gib, I'm going to adopt a baby."

"You're what?" he said, leaning slightly toward her.

"You heard what I said. Her name is Alison, she's fourteen months old and she's absolutely wonderful. As soon as the legal paperwork comes through from the judge, I'll be bringing her home."

Gib got to his feet and stared at the floor as he ran one hand over the back of his neck. He frowned when he looked at Margaret again.

"Margaret, have you really thought this through? I mean, my God, you're talking about diapers, cutting teeth, potty training. Then there's PTA meetings, school plays, *adolescence,* with the slamming of bedroom doors and teary tantrums at the drop of a hat. Babies don't stay cute and cuddly...they become teenagers!''

Margaret smiled. ''I'm aware of that fact, Gib.''

''Why can't you just wait to become a grandmother?'' he said, his voice rising.

Margaret's smile disappeared. ''I'm not attempting to justify my decision, Gib, I'm simply sharing it with you. It's not up for debate, or censure. If you have negative things to say, please keep them to yourself. As for last night...'' Her voice trailed off.

''Yes?'' Gib said, folding his arms over his chest. ''What about last night?''

''I'll cherish the memories of what took place between us, Gib. It was all so special, so beautiful. I don't usually... What I mean is, I'm not in the habit of making love with every man I go out with. I hope you know that. I have no regrets about sleeping with you. None. It was a lovely ending of an era in my life.''

''What in the hell does *that* mean?''

''Why are you getting so angry? I'm being realistic, that's all. I don't expect you, or any man our age, to wish to become involved in the complications of seeing a woman who has a baby. My dating days are over, and I'm accepting that fact.''

''Wait just a damn minute here,'' Gib said slowly, raising one hand. ''Let me make sure I have this straight. You acted out of character by going to bed with me after knowing me such a short length of time?''

"Well, yes, I—"

"But you slept with me because you think that men my age are going to head for the hills upon hearing the news of the arrival of your baby?"

"You're making it sound cheap, tacky and..."

Gib lunged forward and planted his hands flat on the bed on either side of Margaret's hips, trapping her in place.

"Exactly the words I would pick to describe it," he said, a muscle ticking in his jaw. "You used me, Margaret Madison."

"No!"

"Oh, yes. You wanted one last fling, one last roll in the hay, before you were elbow-deep in diapers. Cheap? Tacky? You called it, lady. Was I good enough for you, Margaret? Are you satisfied with your choice of stud for your last go-round?"

"Stop it!"

"I'll stop, all right." He straightened, strode around to the other side of the bed to snatch his shirt from the floor, then shrugged into it. "I'll stop thinking about you...finally...after having you consume my brain space for far too long."

"Gib, please, you're standing in such harsh judgment of me. I didn't set out to sleep with you last night. I simply decided I would do whatever felt right, without weighing and measuring the consequences because—"

"Save it, Margaret," Gib said gruffly. He sat

down on the edge of the bed to put on his shoes and socks. "You're just digging a deeper hole. No matter how prettily you attempt to rationalize what you did, the bottom line is still the same." He got to his feet and picked up his jacket. "You used me. Am I standing in harsh judgment of you for that? Damn straight I am."

He started toward the bedroom door.

"Gib, wait."

"Have a nice day, life. Have a nice baby," he said, none too quietly. "Hell, have a nice whatever you want. You're apparently an expert at doing things your way, with no regard for anyone else's feelings. Goodbye, Margaret."

Margaret leaned forward, nearly losing her grip on the sheet covering her bare breasts. She jerked as she heard the front door of the house slam behind Gib.

Sinking back on the pillow, she leaned her head against the headboard, closing her eyes.

Dear heaven, she thought, what a nightmare, what an ugly scene. She'd never been involved in such a nasty argument, never seen a man so angry and hurt because of *her* actions.

She raised her head and opened her eyes, aware of a queasy feeling in her stomach caused by what had just transpired with Gib.

He was wrong, she thought. She had *not* used him in the manner he was accusing her of.

Margaret pressed trembling fingertips to her temples.

Had she?

No, darn it. She hadn't dragged Gibson McKinley into her bed kicking and screaming. He had been a *very* willing participant in their lovemaking. He certainly hadn't been interested in interviewing her beforehand to determine her motives or any future expectations she might have after their intimacy.

That Gib didn't approve of her whys and wherefores in the light of the new day was *his* problem. She hadn't done one single thing wrong.

Had she?

"Oh-h-h," she said with a moan of frustration.

She flung back the blankets, left the bed and crossed the room to collect clean clothes before heading for the shower.

She was suddenly out of her league, she thought, yanking open a dresser drawer. She'd been hurled into the swinging singles scene and had no idea what the rules of conduct were. Obviously, *her* conduct was not acceptable to Mr. Gibson Playboy McKinley.

She'd bet five dollars that Gib had had his share of one-night stands, but he certainly got his machismo in a rip when he thought he might have been the unsuspecting participant in one.

"Men," Margaret said with a little snort of disgust.

Moments later she was standing under the warm, soothing cascade of water in the shower. As she soaped her body, memories of Gib's hands and lips on her skin assaulted her, and a thrumming heat began to stir deep within her.

Oh, Margaret, don't, she pleaded with herself. Her Cinderella night had ultimately been a disaster. She had to push it from her mind—every detail—and erase Gibson McKinley from her thoughts.

She didn't want any gloomy clouds hovering over her as she began her life with Alison. Nothing was going to mar the joy of bringing her baby home.

Somehow she was going to forget last night *and* the man involved in it.

Somehow.

Chapter Five

On Monday morning Gib sat in his glass box of an office in the center of the newsroom at *The Houston Holler*. The transparent walls afforded him a complete view of the huge room beyond. Blinds had been installed to afford privacy when required.

He was not in a chipper mood. Not even close. After leaving Margaret's house the previous morning, he'd driven home, showered, changed into casual clothes, then prepared a breakfast he had no appetite for.

Margaret's announcement that she was about to adopt a baby and the scene that had followed had replayed in his mind through the entire day and into the tossing-and-turning night.

No amount of firm mental directives had quelled

the vivid pictures plaguing him for the seemingly endless hours.

Gib squeezed the bridge of his nose and shook his head, the motion aggravating a steadily building headache.

Why couldn't he just forget what had transpired between him and Margaret? he asked himself for the umpteenth time. He should simply chalk her up as a woman with a double dose of maternal instincts, and let that be that. She was not, with baby in tow, his cup of tea. The end.

So why in the hell couldn't he do that?

Because, he thought wearily, he couldn't forget making exquisite love with Margaret Madison.

There were also memories of dancing at the restaurant, the ecstasy of holding Margaret in his arms as they swayed to the dreamy music.

He could see Margaret so clearly, so vividly, it was as though she was standing right before him. He could even detect her flowery aroma, hear her lilting laughter, feel the softness of her dewy skin beneath his tingling fingertips.

And her lips?

Man, oh, man, those honey-sweet lips of Margaret's had driven him wild, causing him to seek and capture them time and again.

Margaret had given of herself completely when they'd made love, holding nothing back. She was the quintessential woman, conducting herself with grace, dignity and class in public, then rejoicing in her own femininity in the privacy of the bedroom.

Oh, yes, Margaret was a rare and wonderful find among the multitude of available females he knew. She had it all, everything a man could possibly want, including intelligence, beauty, a sense of humor.

But the list didn't stop when it was supposed to. There was one last description that overshadowed all the others. Forty-six-year-old Margaret was about to become a mother again when she adopted fourteen-month-old Alison.

"Damn it," Gib said, smacking the desk with the palm of one hand.

She needed physical exertion this Monday morning, Margaret decided. That was the solution to relaxing her tight muscles and easing her stress headache. She'd spent a horrendous Sunday, unable to move emotionally past the terribly upsetting scene with Gib.

She'd gone over it, word by angry word, so many times that she'd exhausted herself, while increasing her tension level to the point where she was clenching her teeth.

So many questions had begun to tumble through her mind in a never-ending, echoing maze. She was now a confused, befuddled mess. She didn't know if she was guilty or innocent of Gib's heated accusation that she had used him to have one last, rather reckless fling before settling sedately into her role of mother.

Had she been selfish, thinking only of herself, with no regard for Gib's emotional state? When it came to the singles scene, where Gib operated, she simply didn't know the rules anymore.

Her occasional dates were with an accountant, who lived with and cared for his ailing mother; a doctor, whose patients always came first; and a banker, who was supporting three ex-wives and had no intention of marrying another potential drain on his finances.

She had slept with none of those men, nor had she had any desire to. They were pleasant company for dinner and a movie, an outing to the theater, or a trip to a museum.

There was nothing sexual in her relationships with those men. They asked only for her companionship for a handful of hours, and she certainly didn't have any lingering, unsettling thoughts of them once she was safely home.

Her behavior with Gibson McKinley was foreign territory. She'd listened to some inner voice, and as a result, she'd engaged in lovemaking so exquisite, so beautiful, it truly defied description.

But, oh, dear heaven, the piper she was paying was demanding more than a pound of flesh. She was an emotional wreck, now questioning her conduct, her values, the entire sequence of events with Gib.

She'd apologize to him, Margaret thought as she stepped onto the back deck. If she was certain that she was wrong. But what if she wasn't? What if Gib had been totally unreasonable with his angry accusations? How foolish she would appear if she humbly asked for forgiveness when she had nothing to be sorry for.

"Margaret, shut up," she mumbled. "You're going nuts."

She *had* to quit dwelling on this whole situation. It was over, finished, done. She'd never see Gibson again, and time would dim the awful memories of that final scene in her bedroom.

And time, she thought dryly, had better erase the *very* vivid memories of making love with Gib before she drove herself right out of her ever-loving mind.

Two hours later Margaret sank onto a chair on the deck, glanced down at herself and laughed aloud.

What a grungy person she was. She'd hosed off the deck, managing to spray herself with water in the process, then proceeded to turn herself into a muddy mess by pulling weeds in the flower beds.

She was wet and filthy dirty, but she felt better for it. She'd managed to *not think* about Gib during her labors, her headache had disappeared and her tension was gone. She was tired and ready for a long soak in a fragrant bubble bath.

The sound of the telephone ringing in the kitchen brought Margaret to her feet. She hesitated as she thought of tracking mud on the sparkling kitchen floor, then shrugged and entered the house. Running on her tiptoes to keep her dirty tennis shoes as far away from the floor as possible, she lunged for the receiver on the wall telephone.

"Yes? Hello?" she said, teetering as she came to a halt.

"Margaret?"

"Yes."

"This is Patricia Conway. Are you all right?"

"Yes, I'm fine, Patricia," Margaret said, laughing. "I dashed in the back door, that's all."

"Well, catch your breath...Mother. This is going to be a big day for you and Alison."

Margaret's free hand flew to her heart, splaying on the wet, muddy T-shirt she was wearing.

"Patricia?" she said, almost whispering. "Are you saying... Oh, my gosh. Patricia?"

Patricia laughed in delight. "I love to make these telephone calls. They're one of the high points of my job." She paused. "Margaret, I have in my hand, even as we speak, your certification papers with a judge's signature and an official court seal."

Instant tears filled Margaret's eyes. "Oh, my God, it's finally happened. I can bring Alison home."

"You certainly can, my dear. I've spoken to Alison's foster mother, Maggie, already this morning. How about meeting me at her home at two this afternoon? We'll sign some documents and I'll witness your removing Alison from foster care. All right?"

"Yes!" Margaret yelled. "Oh, Patricia, I'm sorry. I didn't mean to scream in your ear. It's just that... What I mean is..." She sniffled. "Oh, dear."

"I love it," Patricia said. "Your reaction is a joy to hear. Take a deep breath, then have one last look at your neat-as-a-pin home and prepare yourself for the arrival of a bundle of busy-bee energy. Your baby daughter will be exploding onto the scene very soon. I'll see you at two. Bye for now."

"Yes, yes. Goodbye. And thank you. Thank you. Thank…"

Margaret finally realized she was thanking the dial tone and hung up the receiver. She pressed trembling hands to her cheeks, aware suddenly that tears were streaming down her face.

"Alison, oh, Alison, my darling baby, this is it," she whispered aloud. "You're coming home…with me…with Mommy."

Margaret glanced down at her clothes. Laughing and crying at the same time, she tugged off her tennis shoes before hurrying from the sunny room.

At noon on the Rocking B ranch, Blue Bishop entered the kitchen from the mud room in search of his wife, Amy, and some lunch.

Blue was one of the Bishop boys, as they were often referred to. A trio, Blue had a twin brother, Bram, who was married to Glory, as well as an older brother, Tux, married to Nancy. The first Bishop grandchild for Jana-John and Abe Bishop was arriving in December to happy parents-to-be Tux and Nancy.

When the Bishop boys had accomplished their heartfelt goals of finding their forever loves and marrying, sighs of disappointment had been heard from many of the female populace of Houston and beyond.

Before Blue could greet Amy, he realized that she was talking on the telephone mounted on the kitchen wall. As he turned toward the refrigerator to find fixings for a sandwich, he did a double take as he saw Amy brush a tear from her cheek.

"What? What?" he said, striding to Amy's side. "What's wrong?"

"Yes, I understand," Amy said into the receiver. "It makes perfect sense." She sniffled.

"What makes sense?" Blue said.

Amy waved him away. Blue stayed put.

"Oh-h-h, it is so sweet about Boo," Amy said.

"Who's Boo?" Blue said. "Why is it sweet? Why are you crying? Amy?"

"Blue, hush… Yes, he just came in, Mother. He's having a nosy fit here…I'll tell him everything…. My thoughts will be with you at two o'clock."

"Two with Boo?" Blue said.

"I love you, Mom. Bye for now." Amy replaced the receiver and smiled at Blue. "It's so wonderful."

"Right," he said, frowning. "That's why you're crying. I will *not* live long enough to understand the mystery of women and their tears. It's one of the most complicated things on the face of the earth."

"It is not. We simply have different kinds of tears to suit all occasions. It's extremely efficient."

Blue circled Amy's waist with his arms and pulled her close to him.

"I assume since you're smiling that these are happy tears?" Blue said, then kissed one of her cheeks, then the other.

"Yes. My mother is bringing Alison home today. She's going to the foster home at two, signing papers and scooping up my baby sister."

"That's great," Blue said, matching her smile. "I think what your mom is doing is terrific. The whole Bishop clan is excited about this. When can we visit Alison?"

"Well, you heard me say that it made sense. I was referring to my mom's suggestion that we don't overwhelm Alison by going over there today. The move from the foster home will be enough of an adjustment for the baby."

Blue nodded. "Makes sense."

"My mother will report in tomorrow on how the first night went, and we'll discuss visiting. I can hardly wait to see Alison. Oh, this is all so fantastic."

"I thoroughly agree, sweet wife." Blue paused. "Who's Boo?"

"Oh! Well, when my parents were going to bring me home from the hospital after I was born, my father arrived with a small pink stuffed bunny. It was my coming-home gift from my proud new daddy. My mother said he wiggled it at me and said 'Boo.' That became the bunny's name."

"And you, being a three-day-old genius, said, 'Thanks, Dad.'"

Amy laughed. "No, actually I spit up all over his shirt. Anyway, Mom wanted my permission to take Boo with her when she goes to get Alison this afternoon. Mother thought it would be special if Alison and I shared the same coming-home bunny."

"Oh."

"Oh-h-h," Amy wailed, fresh tears filling her eyes. "That is so-o-o sweet."

"Here we go again," Blue said.

"No, I'm not going to cry anymore. You're in here for lunch. I wish I could remember what I was going to fix. I'm so jangled from that telephone call."

"I'll fix our lunch, but..."

"But?"

"I was thinking, Amy. Alison is officially on the scene as of today. Tux and Nancy's baby will be delivered by Santa Claus. Well, it would be nice, you know, for little kids to grow up together."

"Blue Bishop," Amy said, wrapping her arms around his neck, "are you suggesting that we have a baby?"

"Got it in one."

"I see. And when would you like to start working on this project?"

Blue swung Amy up into his arms as though she weighed no more than a feather pillow.

"Now," he said.

"What about lunch?"

"Later. We'll have lunch later."

Blue strode from the kitchen with his precious cargo held safely in his arms.

The next meal that Mr. and Mrs. Blue Bishop ate was supper.

Margaret stood on the porch at Maggie's and pressed one hand flat on her stomach as she drew a steadying breath.

She'd chosen to wear navy slacks, a navy-and-white-striped top and sandals, deciding that casual clothes might help her feel more calm, cool and collected. The plan hadn't worked one iota, if the swarm of butterflies zooming around in her stomach was any indication.

With a less-than-steady hand she reached out to press the doorbell.

"This is it, Boo," she whispered to the faded pink bunny tucked in the side pocket of her purse.

The door was opened by a smiling woman in her early forties.

"Hello, Margaret," Maggie said. "Come in, come in. This is the big day for you and Alison. I'm so happy for you both."

Margaret returned Maggie's smile and entered the living room.

"I'm a nervous wreck," Margaret said, laughing. "I really am."

"Of course you are. I'd worry if you weren't. I heard Alison squeak a few minutes ago as she was waking from her nap. Sit down, won't you? You know that Alison likes to end her nap at her own pace. Patricia should be here any minute."

Margaret sank gratefully onto the sofa, very aware of her trembling knees.

"Isn't this difficult for you, Maggie?" Margaret said. "Alison has been with you for months. It must be so hard to see her leave."

Maggie nodded. "I'll shed a tear or two after you take her, but you must remember that I've been a foster mother for many years. I don't stay blue for long, because I realize the little ones are going to wonderful homes.

"Besides, I'm getting a newborn tomorrow. He's a drug-addicted baby and will require a lot of special attention."

"You're amazing," Margaret said.

"There are those who will say the same about you for adopting Alison."

Margaret laughed. "And some who will think I'm crazy to do this at my age." Gibson McKinley would qualify to be at the top of *that* list. "I refuse to worry about them." So go away, Gib. *Get out of my head.*

The doorbell rang and Maggie hurried to answer the summons. Moments later Patricia came into the room. She was in her early thirties, had a riot of red curls, freckles and a smile that never seemed to falter.

"Papers to sign," Patricia sang out. "Let's get the bureaucracy out of the way. Maggie, I'll be bringing Benjamin to you at ten tomorrow morning. Is that time all right?"

"I'll be ready," Maggie said.

The papers were signed, proper copies given to Margaret and Maggie, and the remainder replaced in Patricia's briefcase.

"All set," Patricia said.

"Then I'll go get your daughter, Margaret," Maggie said.

My daughter, Margaret mentally repeated, feeling sudden tears stinging her eyes. No, she mustn't cry. Tears would upset Alison.

"That cute bunny looks like it has a history," Patricia said.

"This is Boo," Margaret answered, taking the toy from her purse. She quickly explained the story behind the bunny.

"Oh, that's delightful," Patricia said, "and very special."

"Ladies," Maggie said, "may I present Alison Margaret Madison."

And there she was.

Maggie set the toddler on her feet in the middle of the room. She was wearing a yellow sunsuit with yellow socks and white tennis shoes. She had blue eyes and a meager amount of blond hair that stuck straight up in every direction. When she saw Margaret, Alison smiled, revealing four little white teeth, two on the top, two on the bottom.

"Hello, Alison," Margaret said, fighting against joyful tears. "Hello, sweetheart."

Alison toddled across the room and flung herself across Margaret's knees. Margaret lifted her onto her lap and gave her a hug.

"Kitty," Alison said, pointing to Boo.

Margaret gave her the bunny and Alison pressed it to her rosy cheek.

"Kitty," the baby said again.

Patricia laughed. "I think Boo has a new name."

Maggie left the room and returned with a grocery sack. "I have to keep the majority of things in my stash cupboard," she said, "but I send along a few familiar items. Her favorite blanket is in here, her cup, a book and her pajamas.''

"Thank you," Margaret said.

Patricia stood. "I'm due across town to conduct a home study. Ready to go, Margaret?"

Margaret got to her feet, Alison held tightly in her arms. The baby was jabbering to the toy bunny. Maggie gave Alison a kiss on the cheek, Margaret a quick hug, then she flapped her hands at them. "Go, go, before I weep buckets. Be happy, Margaret. Bye-bye, Alison.''

"Kitty," Alison said merrily.

Outside, Patricia said she'd call Margaret in a few days to see how mom and daughter were doing. Margaret buckled Alison into the car seat, and minutes later they were driving away from Maggie's.

"We're going home, Alison," Margaret said, tears in her voice. "I can hardly believe it's really happening, my darling, but we're going home."

At midnight Margaret threw back the blankets, left her bed, then padded barefoot down the hall to the nursery. A night-light cast a soft glow over the room. Margaret moved to the side of the crib to gaze at a sleeping Alison.

The baby was on her side, one hand resting on Boo the bunny. Her lips were slightly parted and her breathing was even and peaceful. Long lashes fanned her cheeks and her funny, adorable hair was in its usual sticking-straight-up disarray.

Margaret smiled gently, then straightened the lightweight receiving blanket covering the toddler.

Sleep well, Alison, Margaret thought. Oh, what a special night this was. Her baby daughter was home, in her own crib, dreaming the dreams of the innocent.

The baby had taken her new surroundings in stride, fussing only at bedtime. Margaret had rocked her to sleep, then held her for another hour before reluctantly placing her in the crib.

Margaret Madison, she told herself, *go to bed and get the rest you'll need to chase this busy bundle tomorrow.* Yes, she was going…in a minute. She just wanted to look at this little miracle one more time before ending the day and tucking it away in her treasure chest of precious memories.

Alison Margaret Madison, her daughter, was home.

Margaret kissed the tip of one of her fingers, then placed it on the baby's lips with a featherlight touch. She turned from the crib, crossed the room, then stopped to look back once more before starting down the hall.

At the doorway to her own room she hesitated as her gaze swept over the bed. Images of Gib rushed into her head, pushing the lingering picture of Alison aside. Heated desire fluttered low in Margaret's body, as vivid details of the exquisite lovemaking shared with Gib assaulted her.

She shook her head and returned to the bed, pulling the sheet over her.

How long would it take, she wondered, before the

memories of Gibson McKinley faded, then were finally gone forever?

When was her body going to be once again under her control, instead of thrumming with desire whenever Gib forced his way into her thoughts?

When would she forget Gibson and the ecstasy they'd shared, the harsh, angry words they'd exchanged?

Margaret rolled onto her stomach, punched her pillow, then wiggled into a comfortable position.

She'd center her thoughts on Alison, she thought decisively. She'd take beautiful Alison with her into the hours of the night.

But when she finally slept, Margaret dreamed of Gibson McKinley.

"And she's smart, too," Amy said. "She really is. Blue and I bought her one of those shape boxes, you know? Alison put the plastic circle in the hole for the circle. Isn't that something, Gib? The other shapes were too tricky, but she *did* do the circle."

Gib nodded and managed to produce a small smile.

Amy had appeared in his office on this rainy Wednesday morning nearly bursting with excitement over her new little sister. She'd been chattering away for ten minutes, hardly coming up for air.

Included in her glowing report of the baby had been endless references to Margaret, the ecstatic new mother. Each mention of Margaret Madison caused the knot in his gut to grow bigger and more painful.

"Even though Mother brought Alison home on Monday afternoon," Amy rattled on, "we didn't visit until yesterday. Mom wanted to give Alison a chance to settle in. The little doll is doing so great, we were able to go see her already. Alison is—"

"Excuse me, Amy," Gib said. "I hate to interrupt you, but I have a meeting in ten minutes and I need to gather my notes."

"Oh, sure, of course," Amy said, smiling. "I got a bit carried away. It's just that I'm so thrilled about my baby sister. You should see my mom, Gib. She's glowing with happiness, actually glowing."

Amy, please, Gib mentally begged, *give me a break.*

He'd made absolutely no progress—none—in his quest to forget Margaret. His weary mind bounced back and forth between images of a naked, sensuous Margaret reaching out to welcome him into her embrace, and the cold reality of the words she'd spoken that made it clear she'd used him for one final fling before motherhood descended.

The last thing he needed was Amy Madison Bishop being a cheerleader in his office, going on and on about the deliriously happy new mother, Margaret, and cuter-than-cute baby Alison.

"Gib," Amy said, leaning forward in her chair. "I know you're pressed for time, so I'll make this quick. I truly believe there are a lot of women out there in my mother's age bracket who are yearning to raise another baby."

"That," Gib said gruffly, "I seriously doubt. What your mother is doing is *not* the norm, Amy."

Amy straightened. "How do you know that?"

"Because I'm a man in that age bracket, remember? Diapers? Night feedings? Potty training? No way. Nope. We've done our stint. It's over, finished. We borrow our grandchildren for an hour or two, send them home, then settle in for a peaceful evening."

"But," Amy said, raising one finger, "you're a man. I'm talking about women here. I want to do an article featuring my mother and Alison. Consider it a public service, Gib. It just might mean that other kids in foster care will find loving homes."

"Amy, your mother doesn't strike me as the type who would want a spotlight on her and that baby. You said yourself that she kept her plans to adopt Alison a secret even from you until the last minute."

Then Margaret dropped her bombshell on Amy *and* on him, Gib thought. Amy might be thrilled down to her socks about Alison, but *he* sure as hell wasn't.

Amy frowned. "You've got a point there." She paused. "Okay, try this. I'll refer to a single woman in her late forties adopting a toddler, without naming names. I'll be letting the readers know that it's possible to do. It won't have as much punch as a story with a picture, but it's still worth writing."

"Yes, all right," Gib said, getting to his feet. "Go with it."

"Great. I'm going to find a free computer in the

newsroom and get some of my ideas down while my mind is buzzing. Okay?''

"Sure."

"Thanks. Bye."

As Amy left the office, Gib frowned. Now that she was staying within view, he'd have to leave, as well, after telling her he had a meeting to attend. The problem was, he had absolutely nowhere to go!

Just after six o'clock Gib walked slowly across the parking lot toward his car. The rain had stopped during the day, leaving the air heavy and humid.

He was restless, edgy, and had no desire to go home to his big, empty house. Lord, the years he'd spent there, struggling to protect Betsy from the truth about—no, forget it. He wasn't traveling down *that* bumpy memory lane.

What a strange mood he was in.

Maybe it was time to sell the house and buy a condo. No, he didn't like the idea of people living so close, and being directly on the other side of his walls.

He needed a vacation. Okay, fine, good plan. Where should he go? Hawaii? The Bahamas? London? Paris? Forget it. A major trip with new things to do and see needed to be shared with someone. There would be no one to turn to and say, "Hey, look at that. Isn't that something?"

Definitely a strange mood.

Was he hungry? No, not really.

Gib unlocked his car, got in and closed the door,

then shoved the key into the ignition. Then he sat there, glaring into space.

One would think, he fumed, that a man who was about to turn fifty would know from years of experience how he preferred to spend a leisurely evening.

Fifty years old. The big five-oh. Half a century. Jeez, that was a long time to have been on this earth.

He'd bet a buck that Margaret Madison wasn't feeling like a forty-six-year-old woman, with fifty on the horizon. Hell, no, she was probably reliving her twenties, when Amy was a baby. Margaret was no doubt zipping around the house, laughing, talking and playing with Alison.

Yeah, well, it would catch up with Margaret. She might be on an emotional high now, after bringing that baby home. But once the newness wore off, Mrs. Madison was going to be exhausted from chasing a busy toddler all day.

Wasn't she?

Gib turned the key in the ignition with more force than was necessary. He drove out of the parking lot and into the heavy rush-hour traffic, not having a clue as to where he was going.

Maybe Margaret *wouldn't* be tired to the bone every night from caring for Alison. He'd read more than one article that stated that when a person was truly happy with what they were doing, their age was incidental, simply a number to use as a reference.

Nice theory, but it didn't hold water. *He* liked his career at the newspaper, but at the moment he felt more like one hundred and fifty, instead of coming up fast on fifty. Cripe.

What in the blue blazes was wrong with him?

"Forget it," he said aloud. "Just forget it. I'm driving myself nuts here."

Wait a minute, he thought. He knew what he would do. He'd go shopping for shirts. That had been his intention the day he'd bumped...literally...into Margaret at the department store. Not only was Margaret Madison refusing to remove herself from his thoughts, it was her fault that he was low on decent shirts.

Since he was headed in the opposite direction from where he wished to shop, it was nearly half an hour later before Gib was wandering through the large, busy store.

He purchased a dozen shirts, added underwear and socks he didn't really need, then continued to roam from one department to the next.

When he found himself in the toy section, he stopped, narrowing his eyes in thought.

Maybe he was going about this all wrong. He didn't seem capable of erasing Margaret from his memory, which could very well be because they had unfinished business. To use the trendy term, he needed closure.

Brilliant. Now he was hitting on all cylinders. He'd see Margaret one last time, reinforce in his mind how she had used him for her own purposes, then be free of the haunting memories she continually evoked. He'd walk away, and that would be that.

And on what pretense was he to get inside the door at Margaret's house? How could he complete his mission without losing face, or appearing to condone Margaret's behavior?

Simple. He'd buy a toy for Alison because she was Amy's baby sister. He'd be there as a thoughtful employer, who was acknowledging a major event in the life of one of his staff members.

McKinley, he thought, walking farther into the toy section, *you're awesome at times.*

With this plan, he would regain control of his mind and body.

With this plan, Margaret Madison would be out of his thoughts and his life forever.

Chapter Six

On Saturday afternoon Margaret sat cross-legged on the living-room floor, stacking plastic blocks into a tower. Alison sat opposite her.

The baby swept a chubby little hand through the air, connected with the blocks and sent them tumbling. She squealed in delight, clapping her hands.

"All gone," Margaret said, smiling. "Okay. I'll do it again."

"Da-da," Alison said, still clapping. "Da-da, da-da, da-da."

"One," Margaret said, putting a block in front of Alison. "Two."

"Da-da," Alison said, wiggling with excitement.

Margaret smiled as she continued to rebuild the tower.

Da-da. Margaret could remember how thrilled Jack had been the first time Amy had said the word. He'd been convinced, as had she, that their daughter, at only a handful of months old, knew exactly who her father was.

Wrong. During the weeks she'd been waiting to bring Alison home, Margaret had read books and magazines on today's child and the new theories on parenting.

One of her discoveries had been an article on various sounds a baby should be able to make in a bell-curve range of age. One of those noises was "da-da," which indicated a certain type of tongue control that a pediatrician would be watching for. It was *not*, at that early age, identifying an actual father.

Oh, well, Margaret thought. There were legions of fathers who had burst their buttons with pride over hearing the coveted "da-da."

Alison knocked over the tower, laughed and clapped, said "da-da" three times, then Margaret began the process of rebuilding.

Alison would never have a father, Margaret realized. There wouldn't be a man to have the title of "Da-da" when the toddler learned to apply names to people.

Would Alison come to resent Margaret for that fact, perhaps during the upheavals of adolescence? Was that one of the negative issues they'd have to deal with together?

There was no way to know, and she refused to worry about it now. They'd take life as it came, cherishing each precious day. Heaven knew there were a multitude of single mothers in society. Alison wouldn't be alone with her fatherless status.

Oh, Margaret, hush, she told herself. She'd covered this issue from top to bottom while weighing the pros and cons of adopting a baby. Why on earth was she rehashing the father topic?

The doorbell rang, startling Margaret from her unwelcome thoughts.

"I'll be right back, sweetheart," she said to Alison.

Margaret got to her feet, crossed the room and opened the front door. Her eyes widened in surprise as she stared at Gibson McKinley, who was standing before her.

Margaret. Gib's mind hummed. She was just as lovely as she'd been in the never-ending images in his mind that had haunted him day and night.

An explosion of heated desire rocketed through his body at the sight of her.

He'd decided not to telephone first, afraid that Margaret would refuse to see him. He'd arrived on her doorstep, a wrapped present under one arm and a concocted story in his mind.

Yes, there he stood, and Margaret Madison was looking at him as though he was an alien creature who had just landed from another planet.

Take charge, McKinley, he ordered himself. He was here on a mission. This visit was going to achieve the closure he needed regarding Margaret.

When he left this house today, he would be free of the spell she'd woven over and around him.

"Hello, Margaret," he said. "May I come in?"

Margaret blinked. "What? Oh. Well...yes, of course." She moved back to allow him to enter.

Gib stepped into the living room and Margaret closed the door. The house was refreshingly cool, the air-conditioning a welcome relief from the hot, humid weather.

Margaret glanced over to where she'd left Alison and the blocks.

"Uh-oh," she said.

Before Gib could speak, Margaret turned and rushed away, disappearing from view down the hall.

Gib frowned in confusion.

"How are you, Gib?" he muttered. "Fine. And you? What do you think of the weather?" His frown deepened. "Damn it, what's going on here?"

In the next moment his grumpy question was answered as Margaret reappeared carrying a smiling, squirming child in her arms.

"You little monkey," Margaret said, laughing. "You headed for trouble the second I turned my back."

She set Alison on her feet. As the toddler caught sight of Gib, who hadn't moved from just inside the door, she sobered and threw her arms around one of Margaret's legs, hanging on tightly.

"Gibson," Margaret said, lifting her chin. "This is my daughter, Alison." There was no hint of a smile on Margaret's face. "Alison Margaret Madison."

His heart, Gib thought incredulously, had done a funny little tap dance when he'd seen Alison. He'd felt a tug, a pull, when he'd looked at the baby.

Lord, she was cute. Her hair, however, had better get its act together before she got to the gazing-in-the-mirror stage, or they'd hear her shrieking in dismay all the way to Toledo.

Alison was staring at him with big blue eyes, while hanging on to Margaret for dear life. She was afraid of him. Damn, he didn't want her to be frightened of him. Why that was so important he had no idea, but it was.

Gib hunkered down, placing the brightly wrapped package before him on the carpet.

"Hello, Alison," he said quietly, smiling as he spoke. "You sure are a pretty girl. This present is for you. What do you think? Do you want to come get it?" He pushed the package forward.

Alison stuck her thumb in her mouth, looked at the gift, then Gib, then the present again.

"That's fine," Gib said. "You think it over. We've got all the time in the world."

Dear heaven, Margaret thought, taking a quick, much-needed breath. She'd forgotten to breathe. She'd been stunned by the fact that Gib had arrived unannounced on her doorstep.

And now? Now she couldn't take her eyes off him. She was mesmerized by the way his faded jeans molded to his thighs as he crouched down. The black knit shirt he wore accentuated his thick dark hair, tanned, rugged features, broad shoulders and chest and...

Margaret, stop it, she admonished herself. She had to remember that Gibson operated in a social scene where she didn't know the rules, or how to play the game. He was there for a definite purpose, and she'd better stay on her guard until she discovered what his motives were.

She should say something to him. But what? Well, she'd ask if he would like to get off the floor and sit down in a chair. That was safe enough.

Before Margaret could speak, Alison released her hold on Margaret's leg and started forward tentatively, her thumb still securely in her mouth. She stopped at the package, looked at it, then halted directly in front of Gib. Popping her thumb out of her mouth, she smiled.

"Kitty," she said, patting Gib on the cheek. "Kitty."

He now knew what the term "his heart melted" meant, Gib thought. His heart was mush, and he was putty in this little doll's hands. Man, oh, man, Alison Margaret Madison was really something.

Alison *Margaret,* his mind echoed. During these minutes while Alison was running roughshod over his emotions, he'd completely forgotten about Margaret.

He was here for a definite purpose: to be able to *leave* with no lingering thoughts or memories of Margaret Madison. He would now deliver his phony spiel about coming on Amy's behalf, as her employer, and get this show on the road.

Gib planted his hands on his thighs and pushed himself up.

Alison immediately raised her arms.

"Up," she said.

"Oh," Gib said, frowning slightly. "Well, I... Okay, kiddo."

He lifted Alison into his arms and inhaled her baby aroma of soap and lotion. She was a solid little bundle in a ruffled sunsuit, and she fit perfectly into the crook of his arm. She looked directly into his eyes and Gib had the disconcerting feeling that Alison could spot a con a mile away.

That was a sight Margaret had never expected to see—Gibson McKinley holding Alison securely in his arms. What a special and lovely picture they made.

Margaret shook her head, blinked and drew another quick, deep breath.

"Gib," she said, sweeping one arm through the air. "Would you like to sit down?"

Gib bent over, scooped up the present, then crossed the room to settle onto the sofa with Alison on his lap. He placed the gift on the cushion next to him. Margaret sat down in an easy chair.

"Why are you here?" she said. "That sounded rather rude, I guess, but I'm surprised to see you, considering the circumstances of the last time we were together."

Alison patted Gib on the cheek again.

"Doggy," she said. "Kitty."

Gib chuckled.

A flutter of heat stirred low in Margaret's body as she heard the sensuous, male sound of Gib's throaty chuckle.

"Well, I've been a cat and a dog so far," Gib said, smiling. "What's next, Alison?"

The baby clapped her hands.

"Mum-mum," she said happily.

Oh, Alison, please, Margaret silently begged. *Don't do the da-da thing, sweetheart.* Gib was from the old school of men who would believe it was a title directed solely toward him.

"Da-da!" Alison shouted.

Oh, good grief, Margaret inwardly moaned.

"Alison is just making noises," she said quickly. "She really doesn't have a handle yet on actually applying names to people, or things. They're all just sounds to her, baby chatter. She doesn't think you're a kitty, or a dog, or her... What I mean is, don't pay any attention to..." Margaret paused and cleared her throat. "Would you like some iced tea?"

"That would hit the spot," Gib said, smiling.

Margaret nearly jumped to her feet. "Good. I'll go get it. Sugar? Lemon? It's sun tea."

"Texas sun tea is sweet and perfect just as it is."

"Dandy," she said, hurrying across the room.

"And you, Alison," Gib said, "are a Texas baby, so that makes you sweet and perfect just as *you* are."

Heavenly saints, Margaret thought, her step faltering. What a wonderful thing for Gib to have said.

Alison was a sweet, perfect Texas baby? Oh, damn the man. Why was he being so nice? And why was he here?

Margaret zoomed into the kitchen, then stopped dead in her tracks. She pressed her hands flat onto her stomach and drew a deep breath, letting it out slowly to the count of ten.

She had to calm down, she told herself. When Alison had said da-da, the baby's blithering idiot of a mother had started spieling gibberish, as though she didn't have a brain in her head.

Margaret walked forward slowly and began to prepare a tray of refreshments.

Stall, Margaret, she thought. Alison was perched happily on Gib's lap, and he had enough experience as a *da-da,* for Pete's sake, to make certain a toddler didn't wander off and get into possibly dangerous mischief.

She had to get her act together. This was her home, her turf, and she was in control.

Her flustered, ridiculous performance had been embarrassing, but it was over. When she returned to the living room, she'd be polite but cool, pleasant but rather aloof. If she had to, she'd stick her nose in the air and act borderline snooty.

She still didn't know what Gib wanted, but what *she* wanted was for him to march his gorgeous self back out the door and disappear.

She couldn't deal with his presence, with seeing him again, with the heated desire that was consuming her from merely being in the same room with him.

And, oh, the memories of their exquisitely beautiful lovemaking were flitting before her mind's eye, scene after vivid, sensuous scene, haunting and taunting her.

Enough was enough. She was going to demand an explanation for Gib's unannounced arrival, then hustle him out the door.

As for herself, she'd say as little as possible. She had no intention of giving Gib one clue that he'd thrown her for a loop. Nor was she going to let on that she was so inexperienced, so naive about the social conduct rules of the singles scene that she had no idea whatsoever if she owed him an apology for her behavior on the night they'd been together.

There, Margaret thought, picking up the tray. She had it all straightened out, knew her plan of action.

And she certainly hoped that Gib was very thirsty. The sooner he finished his tea, the quicker this nerve-racking visit of his could be ended. The Madison refreshment stand was *not* offering refills of empty glasses.

When she reentered the living room, she saw Alison sitting on the floor, banging on a toy typewriter. Gib was leaning forward to watch, his elbows propped on his knees, his hands laced loosely together.

"Alison is certainly enjoying your lovely gift," Margaret said, forcing a cheerful tone to her voice. She set the tray on the coffee table. "Thank you for thinking of her, Gib."

Gib straightened and sank back against the cushions of the sofa.

Everything was proceeding just as he'd hoped. He now had the exact lead-in he'd wished for. The toy typewriter had been a genius choice of a present.

"Well, Alison is Amy's sister," he said, "so a typewriter seemed appropriate. Who knows? Alison just may be on the staff of *The Holler* somewhere in the far distant future."

He reached out and picked up one of the glasses of tea.

"Amy is so excited about Alison that I..." His voice trailed off, and he frowned, then took a swallow of tea.

Margaret sat down in her chair. "You what?"

Come on, Gib, he directed himself, *do your thing.* He wanted to make it clear that he wasn't here to see Margaret, that he wasn't forgetting or forgiving her self-centered actions of the previous Saturday night.

"I...um..." he went on. "What I mean is, Amy is thrilled about Alison, but I wanted *you* to know that I'm pleased that *you're* happy about your new daughter and the life-style you've chosen for yourself."

What! his mind hammered. Where had all *that* come from? That wasn't what he'd planned to say, not even close.

Damn it, if he believed in such things, he'd certainly be convinced that Margaret *was* a spell weaver, and had magical powers of some sort that rendered a man incapable of maintaining command of his mind...and body.

"I see," Margaret said. She took a sip of tea, then replaced the glass on the tray. "Alison, would you like some juice?"

Alison ignored the question as she continued to poke, prod and bang on the brightly colored plastic typewriter. Margaret redirected her gaze to Gib.

"Am I to assume," she said, remembering to lift her chin, "that you're apologizing for the harsh words you hurled at me the last time we were together?"

"No!" Gib inwardly cringed at the loud volume of his voice. "No," he said quietly. "The way you used me for your own purposes can't be swept under the rug, Margaret. I'm still very angry about that. I'm separating Alison from what happened between us."

"That's not possible to do," Margaret said, delighted with her frosty tone of voice. "My actions stemmed from the pending arrival of Alison."

Gib thunked his glass back onto the tray.

"Why are you making this so difficult?" he said, his brows knitted in a heavy frown. "I brought Alison a gift to welcome her, and to wish you well. End of story. Okay? Have you got that? The issue of you, me, your one-night stand, your last fling, is unfinished business."

"Wrong," Margaret said, getting to her feet. "It's finished, and so is your visit. I'd like you to leave, Gibson. You conveniently forget that you were a willing partner in the intimacy we shared.

"If you're angry regarding my motives, that's *your* problem. I will not apologize for something I'm not thoroughly convinced was inappropriate behavior. *I* have no regrets about that night. Our lovemaking was incredibly beautiful, it was so..."

She waved one hand in the air.

"Never mind," she went on. "Just go. I will *not* subject my child to the sound of people quarreling in her home. Goodbye, Mr. McKinley."

Gib stared at Margaret for a long moment, his frown fading slowly, changing into a slight smile.

"Yes, it was," he said quietly.

"Pardon me?"

"Our lovemaking, Margaret. It *was* very, very beautiful."

"Gibson, look, there's no point in discussing that, or anything else. I'm not accustomed to confrontations. They're extremely upsetting. I think it would be best to forget that we...well, that we ever met."

"You're probably right," Gib said, then sighed and shook his head. "However, you're not that easy to erase from my memory. Can you just push a button and forget me, forget what we shared?"

Margaret sank back onto her chair.

"No," she said dismally. "But in time... Yes, in time I'm sure I will."

"You said you have no regrets about making love with me."

Margaret looked directly at Gib. "No, I don't. It was a special night. Gib, I find it hard to believe that you haven't had one-night stands, to use your term.

I continually see your picture in the society section of your own newspaper with a different woman on your arm in every photograph. I was just one more in a long line, so your anger is baffling."

"The truth be known," he said, "it's confusing the hell out of me, too." He glanced quickly at Alison, who was still engrossed in her typewriter. "I'm sorry. I won't swear in front of Alison again."

He paused, gathering his thoughts. "I'd hate to believe," he said, "that my anger is a power thing, an issue of control. If it stems from the fact that I didn't call the shots about one night, or a dozen nights, with you, it doesn't say a heck of a lot about my character."

"Do tell," Margaret said with an indignant little sniff.

"No," he said, shaking his head. "I'm not that shallow, or that hung up on a machismo image. Our night together was far different from anything I've experienced before. Emotions were involved in our lovemaking, with a depth, an intensity, that was rather unsettling. Because of that, I believe I was more hurt than angry over your dismissal of me."

He leaned forward and made a steeple of his fingers as he propped his elbows on his knees.

"Margaret, you said yourself that we shared something incredibly beautiful. Don't you want to know why it was so special? Don't you want to discover exactly what this is that's happening between us? You also said you had no desire to marry again. Well, neither do I. That, however, doesn't mean there isn't a foundation here for a possible relationship that's very rare.''

"Aren't you forgetting something, Gibson?'' Margaret said.

"Like what?''

"I have a fourteen-month-old baby. She's not a grandchild I give back after spoiling her for a few hours. Alison is my daughter, twenty-four hours a day.''

"You're right,'' he said, frowning. "I forgot about Alison for a moment. I—''

"Drink,'' Alison said.

"Here's your cup, Alison,'' Margaret said. "Come over to Mommy.''

Alison pushed herself to her feet and went to the coffee table. As she reached out to grasp her cup, she knocked over Margaret's glass of iced tea, flooding the tray.

"Oops,'' Margaret said. She handed Alison the cup, then stood. "I'd better clear this away before she decides to splash in the lake she made. Do you want to finish your tea, Gib?''

"No. No, thank you.''

Margaret lifted the tray and made her way carefully across the room, so as not to spill the liquid onto the carpeting.

Twenty-four hours a day, Gib mentally repeated. That was exactly what it took to be a mother, a father, a family. And, no, thank you very much, he'd pass.

But, damn it, this visit to Margaret's, seeing her

again, was definitely *not* going to accomplish what he'd intended it to. He wasn't going to be able to walk out the front door free of the spell-weaving memories of Margaret Madison.

So, now what?

There was only one solution, he supposed. He'd have to hang around a while longer, until he'd reached a saturation point of diapers and spilled glasses of iced tea. When Alison's presence became all-consuming, exhausting, the magic of Margaret would be buried beneath the constant care of the busy baby.

And that, *finally*, would be that.

Alison smacked her cup onto the coffee table and smiled at Gib.

"Kitty," she said.

"Okay, I'm a kitty," Gib said, smiling.

"Da-da," Alison said.

Cross that one off your list, kiddo, Gib thought. His daughter was a grown woman with children of her own. The last thing he ever intended to be was Alison Margaret Madison's daddy!

Chapter Seven

I'll call you soon.

During the next few days Gibson McKinley's parting words on Saturday afternoon echoed in Margaret's head when she least expected them, causing her to frown each time she heard them.

By late Tuesday morning she was furious with herself, as she realized she was registering a sense of anticipation whenever the telephone rang, then a flicker of disappointment when the caller wasn't Gib.

Stern lectures delivered to herself regarding her adolescent behavior did nothing to dim the rush she felt when the telephone shrilled its summons.

Also building within her was a maze of confusion. There was no room in her life for a man, she told herself over and over.

All of her physical and emotional energies were being directed toward Alison. Even more, a swinging bachelor like Gib McKinley wasn't even her type, whether she was tending to a baby or not.

Margaret sat down at the kitchen table with a mug of hot tea. She cradled the mug in both hands as she propped her elbows on the table. Gazing out the bay window at the lush green grass and vibrant flowers in the backyard, she sighed.

Why, why, why, she asked herself yet again, was she allowing Gibson to complicate her life at a time when she wished only to devote herself to her new daughter?

Why couldn't she simply dismiss the man completely from her mind?

Why did she dream of Gib at night, often awakening in the darkness to feel desire stirring within her body?

"Why?" Margaret said aloud. "Because I made a terrible mistake."

The Cinderella night with Gib was backfiring to the maximum. Her inability to erase memories of him was no doubt due to her out-of-character behavior. Her go-for-the-gusto attitude, which had resulted in her making love with Gibson, was now coming back to haunt her.

Her subconscious was apparently working overtime to justify what she had done. She didn't sleep with a man unless he was special, an intricate part of her life. Therefore, her mind was clinging to images of Gib, pushing him into the spotlight, declaring him to be important.

Well, she thought, she'd finally figured it out. The next question was what she was going to do about it.

Yes, making love with Gib had been beautiful, but, no, he was *not* an important part of her existence. She didn't want him in her life at all. Her raison d'être, and happily so, was Alison.

I'll call you soon.

Margaret set the mug of tea on the table and narrowed her eyes.

All right, Gibson, call me…the sooner the better. If she couldn't scold herself into forgetting him, she'd have to take a different approach. She needed to see him one last time, behave as she normally would while in his presence, firmly reinforce that she had no place or desire for a man in her life, and that would be that.

She sighed again.

She really hated the idea that she might yet come to regret her Cinderella night. It had been so wonderful, such ecstasy. But a lifetime of straitlaced behavior and code of conduct was beginning to crush her beautiful memories. She just wasn't cut out to be a one-last-fling woman.

Margaret stiffened, listening as she cocked her head to one side.

Alison was awake and babbling to herself after her morning nap. In another few minutes the baby would be standing in her crib, demanding to be rescued.

After placing the mug in the dishwasher, Margaret headed toward Alison's bedroom. As she crossed the living room, her gaze fell on the plastic typewriter where it lay among the other strewn toys.

At the moment the typewriter was the baby's favorite toy. Alison continually plunked it on Margaret's lap, then banged merrily on the noisy keys.

And every time Margaret looked at the brightly colored toy, she saw the image of a smiling Gibson McKinley.

She glared at the toy typewriter, then hurried on her way.

Late that afternoon Amy entered Gib's office.

"Hi, boss," she said.

Gib looked up, then tossed the pen he was holding onto the top of the stack of papers in front of him.

"Hello, Amy, what brings you into town from the wilderness?"

Amy laughed. "The Rocking B isn't *that* far outside the city limits." She extended some papers toward Gib. "I brought in my story on single adoptive mothers. I touched on the older-mom angle, too. My mother read it and was very pleased with how I presented the subject."

Gib took the papers, flipped through them, then frowned, pulling one sheet free.

"Cake, punch, butter mints," he read. "Balloons, centerpiece..."

"Oh, for heaven's sake," Amy said, "how did

that get in there? That's my list for the surprise baby shower for my mother.''

Gibson handed her the paper. "Oh?" He got to his feet and came around the desk, sliding one hip onto the front edge. "Sit down, Amy. Make yourself comfortable. Would you like some coffee?"

"No, thank you, and there's no need for me to sit. I just wanted to drop off that story."

"You don't have to rush off, do you? I'd like to hear about the plans for the baby shower you're organizing for your mother."

"You would?" Amy sank onto one of the chairs. "You're asking about the details of a baby shower?" She eyed Gib warily. "Why?"

"There you go," Gib said, producing one of his best smiles. "That's just one of the things that makes you such an excellent reporter…your curiosity. That question of *why* was right on the mark." He leaned forward slightly. "You said the shower is to be a surprise?"

"Yes," she said, still looking at Gib suspiciously. "I know my mother. She'd say that showers are for young, first-time moms. I've talked to a lot of her friends, and they all agree that Mother should have a fuss made over her like anybody else. Everyone is so happy for her, because they know that *she's* happy."

"Makes sense. So, is this shower just for women and kids?"

"Well, no. Blue pouted when I said it was a woman thing, and Tux told Nancy he wanted to meet

Alison and practice talking to a little girl. They're expecting a baby in December, you see. Then Bram jumped in and said he didn't want to be left out of the festivities.''

Amy laughed and shook her head. ''Those Bishop boys are really something. Anyway, there are couples who have known my mother for years, knew my father, as well. Then there are the ladies who do volunteer work with my mom and… Well, the party is getting bigger by the minute.''

''Where are you going to have it?''

''The Rocking B is too far out of town to ask people to come there. Bram and Glory are living in an apartment while they look for land to buy, so Bram can build their house. So we decided to have a backyard deal at Tux and Nancy's home.''

Gib nodded. ''Sounds good, except it's a tad warm these days.''

''We'll have it early evening after the sun goes over. Tux said he'd string pretty fairy lights all around. It's going to be a week from this Saturday night, and so far I have things organized to the max. If it rains, I'll die.''

''It wouldn't dare.'' Gib cleared his throat. ''Surprise parties are difficult to pull off. How are you going to get your mother and Alison to the house at exactly the right time?''

Amy frowned. ''I haven't figured that out yet. If Nancy and Tux invite her for a Bishop clan barbecue, or whatever, Mother might arrive too early. She hates to be late for anything. Plus, she'd want to help out in the kitchen."

"Look, Amy, why don't I take care of getting your mother and Alison to Tux and Nancy's place when you want them there?"

"You? But..."

"I met your mother at your wedding, remember? And I... Did she happen to mention that we went out to dinner and dancing recently? Or that I stopped by with a gift for Alison?"

"No, she didn't say a word."

Well, damn, Gib thought. Thanks a hell of a lot, Margaret. That certainly indicated how high on Margaret Madison's list of things to share with Amy that *he* was. Chalk up one pop to the male ego chops delivered by Mrs. Madison.

"You've been out on a date with my mom?" Amy said, raising her eyebrows. "Then visited again to take Alison a present?"

"Well, yes, I did. I gave Alison a noisy toy typewriter that she really liked. Your baby sister sure is a cutie-pie."

"Yes, she is. This is very interesting. My boss is dating my mother."

"I wouldn't put it exactly like that," Gib said, frowning.

"Why not?"

"Because your mother is concentrating on Alison, not on social outings with men." Gib paused. "So, do I get the assignment of maneuvering your mom to the right place at the right time?"

"Sure. That will be one more thing I can cross off my long list. I'll give you all the details later." Amy got to her feet. "You do realize that if you bring Mother and Alison, I'll be counting on you to take them home and help tote the gifts. You'll have to actually attend a baby shower, Gib."

"No problem."

"You really don't strike me as the baby shower attendee type."

"Amy, I'm just full of surprises," he said, smiling. "I'll be looking forward to this event."

"Interesting," she repeated. "Well, I'm off. Bye for now."

"Say hello to Blue for me," Gib said cheerfully. "Goodbye, Amy."

Gib watched Amy leave, then resisted the urge to punch his fist in the air and holler "Yes!" Having a glass cubicle for an office definitely had its disadvantages at times. He settled for a grin as he sat back down in his chair.

Convincing Margaret to go out with him and to bring Alison along was going to be a challenge, he thought, and he certainly enjoyed a challenge.

And maybe seeing Margaret again would accomplish his goal of breaking the strange spell she'd cast over him. He'd be helping Amy at the same time by delivering an unsuspecting Margaret to the surprise baby shower.

He was actually going to attend a baby shower? Grim. Well, he'd survive. An entire evening of cute gifts, kids running around and women talking nonstop about colic, potty training and their little darlings' antics would go a long way toward his reaching an overdose level of the Alison and Margaret duo.

The whole scenario was perfect.

Feeling in charge, and very, *very* smug, Gib picked up his pen and got back to work.

The week had flown by, Margaret thought on Sunday evening. Her days were so full and busy that one seemed to flow into the next.

She settled onto the sofa with the newspaper, having learned that it was much better to wait until Alison was asleep before reading *The Holler*, rather than attempting to read with the help of busy little hands.

It had been a marvelous week, she mused, scanning the stories on the front page of the paper. She and Alison had done so many things together. The curious and excited baby had made even the most mundane chore of shopping for groceries a new adventure.

Of course, Margaret thought, smiling, it also took twice as long to accomplish simple tasks like putting the groceries away, or vacuuming the house, due to Alison's "assistance."

Margaret sighed in contentment as she finished the front section of the paper, then reached for the next.

"Oh," she said aloud as she stared at the photograph before her.

It was Gib, she realized, looking drop-dead gorgeous in a tuxedo. And there, with her arm laced through his and her head tilted toward Gib's, was a beautiful young woman in a slinky dress that accentuated her extremely voluptuous breasts.

Margaret read the caption beneath the picture. Apparently the owner of *The Houston Holler* had been among those attending a charity dinner for a new wing for one of Houston's hospitals. No mention was made as to the identity of the woman in the picture.

"She's young enough to be his daughter," Margaret muttered with a sniff of disgust.

She turned the page, looked at the columns and ads, then flipped back to the photograph. Frowning, she moved the paper closer for a better look.

Wait a minute, she thought. There was a man's hand coming in from the side of the photo and resting on the young woman's back. There was also a wedding band on the woman's ring finger.

Well, fancy that. The lush young thing was obviously married to the man not shown. The photographer had probably told the woman to inch closer for a group shot, and the society section editor had cropped the picture to fit the space available.

She'd figured that all out just like a detective, Margaret thought with a decisive nod.

She tossed the paper onto the stack on the cushion next to her and stared into space.

All right, Detective Madison, the next dilemma to decipher was why on earth she was so pleased to discover that Gib had not been on a date with the beautiful young woman. Why was she so happy at the prospect that he might very well have attended the event alone?

Why was she now sitting in her living room *smiling,* for Pete's sake?

Oh, that Gibson McKinley was a menace, he really was. He hovered in her mind like a pesky bee, causing desire to pulse low in her body and her heartbeat to quicken.

She could still see in such vivid detail Gib sitting on the sofa with a smiling Alison on his lap. How right they had looked, how perfect together.

"Oh, Margaret," she said aloud, pressing her fingertips to her temples. "Why are you doing this?"

She was so angry with her lack of ability to erase Gibson from her memory. And she was frightened, too, about the strange hold he seemed to have over her.

She didn't want this intrusion into her happiness with Alison. She didn't need this unsettling disruption of her contentment and peace of mind.

I'll call you soon.

Once again, Gib's words echoed in Margaret's head.

What was Gib's definition of "soon"? she wondered. She didn't know and, therefore, it was time to take matters into her own hands. She'd decided she needed to see Gib one last time. Why did she have to wait for *him* to call *her?*

Margaret got to her feet and headed for the kitchen and the cupboard where she now kept the telephone book out of the reach of Alison's busy little fingers.

Ten minutes later Margaret lifted the receiver from the kitchen wall telephone and punched in the numbers she'd memorized. A knot tightened in her stomach as she heard the ringing begin on the other end...once, twice, three times.

"Hello?"

"Gibson?" Margaret said, hoping her voice sounded strong and steady, but seriously doubting it. "This is Margaret Madison. I hope I'm not disturbing you."

"No, not at all. This is a nice surprise. How are you? And how is Alison?"

"We're fine, just fine. We're busy, settling into a routine, discovering what does and doesn't work."

"Such as?"

Such as? Margaret mentally repeated. She had been chattering, for heaven's sake. She hadn't called Gib to be interviewed on the progress she was making with Alison.

"Margaret?"

"Oh. Well, such as allotting extra time for folding the laundry and putting away groceries when I have Alison's help."

Gib chuckled.

A shiver slithered down Margaret's spine.

"I also learned, the hard way," she went on, "to wait until Alison is asleep before I attempt to read *The Holler*." Margaret paused. "Speaking of which, I saw your picture on the society page. You certainly do keep busy."

"It's part of the public relations hoopla for the

newspaper. That photograph failed to show the administrator of the hospital, who was next to his wife. She and I appear to be attending the event together, which certainly wasn't the case."

She'd already figured that out, Margaret thought smugly.

"Oh?" she said. "I guess I didn't give it much thought." *Some* thought, but not *much* thought. "Gib, I really didn't call to chitchat."

"Why not? This is very pleasant."

Damn him, Margaret thought, pressing one hand to her forehead. She was losing control of this conversation. Gibson was so darn smooth, slick, and he always seemed to turn things in the direction *he* wished them to go. Well, not this time. *She* had called *him.*

"Gib, I was wondering if you'd care to join me and Alison for a home-cooked dinner tomorrow night?"

"I'd be delighted, but unfortunately I have a supper engagement with an important advertiser, who likes to be wined and dined occasionally in exchange for his loyalty to *The Holler.*"

"I see. Well, how is Tuesday night for you?"

"Not good. In fact, this whole week is brutal. I'll tell you what, Margaret. Why don't I take you and Alison to a family restaurant on Saturday night? I'm sure you want Alison to become comfortable eating in places other than her own kitchen."

"Well, yes, I do, but—"

"Great. I'll pick you two up about six-thirty on Saturday. All right?"

"I—"

"There's someone at my door, Margaret. Saturday? Six-thirty?"

"Yes, but—"

"Wonderful. I'll see you then. Goodbye."

As the dial tone buzzed in Margaret's ear, she replaced the receiver slowly, then just stood there, a rather bemused expression on her face.

Not hindered by his glass-enclosed office, Gib punched his fist into the air and yelled a resounding "Yes!" into the quiet room.

Lord, he was good. Margaret had played right into his hands. He was now all set to get her and Alison to the baby shower, per Amy's instructions.

Gib's grin changed into a frown in the next instant.

Back up, McKinley, he ordered himself.

He was so full of himself over manipulating the outing with Margaret on Saturday night that he was forgetting an important question. Why had Margaret Madison invited him to dinner at her house in the first place?

Why was the woman, who had said it would probably be best if they'd never met, suddenly seeking his company to share a meal with her and her new daughter?

What was going on in the intriguing, complicated mind of the beautiful Mrs. Madison?

Chapter Eight

Saturday started out on the wrong foot, and went from bad to worse.

Alison, Margaret decided early on, was in a mood that was less than adorable.

The baby had begun the day by stripping her crib of the blanket, sheet, mattress pad and teddy bear, dumping them all over the side rail onto the floor. Her pajamas and a very soggy diaper had followed.

A naked, wailing Alison had greeted Margaret when she'd entered the nursery.

Breakfast had been a total disaster. Alison had clamped her mouth shut and refused to take one bit of cereal from the Snoopy spoon. A cup of milk was sent flying, the contents hitting Alison, Margaret, the floor and two kitchen cupboards.

While Margaret cleaned up the milky mess, a freed-from-her-high-chair Alison upended the kitchen trash basket.

"Uh-oh," Alison said.

"You've got that straight," Margaret answered. She scooped the toddler into her arms before Alison could delve into the treasures of the trash. "You're full of the dickens today, aren't you, young lady?"

Alison clapped her hands merrily. "Mum-mum. Pretty. Pretty."

Margaret marched into the living room and set Alison on the floor among her toys.

"Don't try to butter me up," Margaret said. "You play with your toys while I dig through the debris in the kitchen."

"Toy," Alison said, reaching for the typewriter.

Five minutes into restoring order to the kitchen, Margaret heard Alison shriek, the sound registering the baby's frustration, not pain. Hurrying back into the living room, Margaret found the human dynamo stuck beneath the sofa cushions with her trusty typewriter.

And on it went.

When Alison was finally taking a late-morning nap, Margaret finished repairing the damage done by her busy daughter, then sank gratefully onto a chair at the kitchen table with a mug of cinnamon tea.

"Oh, my," she said aloud, laughing, "how could I have forgotten about days like this one? Amy had her share of them, too."

Margaret swept her gaze over the kitchen, nodding in satisfaction that everything was back to normal.

If Alison's attitude remained as it was for the duration of the day and evening, Gib was going to be in for megatrouble when he took them out to dinner.

Whenever Amy had been a holy terror upon awakening at dawn, the destruction of hearth, home and mother's nerves had lasted until a fresh start the next morning.

Alison's behavior throughout the afternoon would be a definite clue as to the disaster dining at a restaurant might be that night.

Margaret frowned as she took a sip of tea.

She'd had the whole week to attempt to figure out why Gib had invited her and Alison to dinner, but had come up with no answer to the perplexing question.

She knew why *she* had asked Gib to join them for a meal, but what were *his* motives?

Gib's invitation made absolutely no sense, considering that he'd made it very clear he was still angry and hurt over her alleged using of him for her own selfish purposes.

Margaret shook her head.

Men were such complicated creatures. Even after many years of marriage to Jack, there had been numerous occasions when his actions, or way of thinking, had been a complete mystery.

What had Gib's marriage been like? she mused. It had ended so tragically when his wife was killed in an automobile accident, and Gib had said he never intended to marry again.

Perhaps, like her, he felt the near perfection he'd had in wedded bliss could never be reached again.

Well, it was none of her business why Gib had resolved to remain single, she thought, draining the mug of tea.

In fact, nothing he did would concern her after tonight. Going out with Gib this final time would end her preoccupation with him. This evening would enable her to at last erase Gib from her mind.

The plan would work.

It just had to.

"Oh, no, you don't," Margaret said, plopping Alison back in the center of her bed. "You stay right there where I can see you while I finish getting dressed. Let's sing a song. Okay?"

"'Kay. 'Kay. 'Kay," Alison yelled.

Margaret belted out a very off-key rendition of "I'm a Little Teapot," which thoroughly delighted Alison. While singing the ditty for the third time, Margaret managed to dress in white slacks, a deep rose silk blouse and sandals.

Alison wore a pale blue pinafore with bunnies in perky hats prancing around the hem of the skirt.

"What do you think, Alison?" Margaret said, studying her reflection in the full-length mirror. "Your mommy doesn't look so bad, considering I'm one of the older moms your sister Amy wrote about in *The Holler.*"

"Kitty," Alison said.

"Go for 'pretty,'" Margaret said, laughing. "After the day you put me through, you owe me one."

"Doggy," Alison said.

"Thanks a bunch." Margaret lifted the baby into her arms and hugged her. "I love you, love you, love you," she said, nuzzling Alison's neck.

The toddler squealed and giggled, then began to wiggle, demanding to be put down. The moment her feet touched the floor, Alison headed for the bedroom door.

"And she's off and running!" Margaret laughed and hurried after her daughter.

Gib combed his hair in front of the mirror in the master bathroom of his house. He set the comb on the edge of the sink and leaned forward, frowning at his reflection.

Did that face look fifty years old? he wondered. What was fifty supposed to look like? He sure had a lot of crow's-feet by his eyes. Were they from squinting against the Houston sun or were they produced by his age?

There was more gray at his temples than there had been a couple of months ago. How long would it be before his whole head resembled a snow-covered mountain?

Fifty. Cripe. Forty-nine hadn't sounded bad at all. He hadn't given it any thought the entire year. But now...

If he was really taking Margaret and Alison out to

dinner, instead of delivering them to the surprise
baby shower, the people in the restaurant would au-
tomatically assume he was Alison's grandfather.

Well, no, maybe not. Margaret appeared younger
than forty-six, and women were having babies later
in life these days. There just might be some among
the observers who would think he and Margaret were
Alison's parents, not her grandparents.

Yes, that was certainly possible. Mom, Dad and
the baby were having dinner out at a family restaurant.

Gib smiled and nodded. In the next instant he
glowered at his image.

Why was he spending time and energy thinking
about such nonsense? He was *not* Alison's father, nor
did he wish to be. He was *not* Margaret's husband,
nor did he wish to be. And he was *not* yet fifty, damn
it, nor did he wish to be.

"Fine, McKinley," he said to the mirror. "That's
a whole list of what you don't wish to be, but what
do you really *want?*"

With a snort of self-disgust, he turned and strode
out of the bathroom, smacking the light switch as he
passed it. In the bedroom he sat down on the edge
of the bed, slipped on his shoes, then bent over to
tie them.

He hadn't thought about his life-style in years, he
fumed. He just lived it, took it as it came, no questions asked.

This was all Margaret's fault. All that talk about
taking inventory of his life at his milestone birthday,

and he was actually doing it. Ridiculous. His existence was perfectly fine just as it was, thank you very much.

Wasn't it?

Gib got to his feet slowly, then swept his gaze over the large bedroom.

Masculine to the maximum, he thought. There wasn't one feminine frill, no hint of a woman's touch. He'd gradually removed evidence of Elizabeth's existence from the entire house, during the years since her death. There was nothing left of her here, except haunting, painful memories he refused to embrace.

Gib left the room, made his way along the hall, then down the stairs. He felt strange, rather disoriented, as though he was seeing his house, his home, his haven, for the first time.

It was very big, this structure. And very, *very* quiet. The cleaning crew that came in once a week kept it picture-perfect neat, not a thing out of place, like a showroom in a store.

Gib stood still in the enormous living room, the only sound the echo of his own heartbeat in his ears.

In Margaret Madison's home laughter must ring through the air like enchanting wind chimes, the laughter of a contented mother playing with her happy baby.

There was no model-home neatness at Margaret's; the living-room floor was strewn with brightly colored toys. It was a room of enchantment and discovery for Alison as she learned, with wonder and awe, what happened when she pushed the buttons, or pulled strings, or banged on something like a miniature toy typewriter.

There was a world of firsts, of beginnings, at Margaret Madison's, and a multitude of events that would unfold as Alison grew. The little girl would ride a bike for the first time, start school, learn how to spell her name, be introduced to the wondrous magic of being able to read.

Gib drew in a deep breath and let it out slowly, realizing he was shaken.

His house had an aura of endings, of things that had been but were now over, finished. There was nothing to discover here, to anticipate, except the sameness of tomorrows that would flow one into the next, clicking off time on an unseen calendar that represented the rest of his life.

Gib dragged both hands down his face, then spun around and started toward the door.

He was thoroughly depressing himself, he thought as he left the house. He'd had quite enough of the taking-inventory-at-fifty routine. His house was fine. His life was fine. Everything was fine. He was stirring up imaginary emotional problems by dwelling on things that didn't need dwelling on.

As he drove away from the house, he vowed that tonight was the *last* time he intended to see Margaret. As crazy as it was, the unconventional life-style *she'd* chosen for herself at her age was having a negative effect on *his* sense of well-being.

If the memories of Margaret continued to hover in

his mind, he'd ignore them until they disappeared due to lack of attention.

He'd had enough, far too much, of Margaret Madison turning his serene existence upside down.

Gib flipped on the radio and refused to let his mind wander as he drove the miles to Margaret's.

Gibson McKinley in gray slacks and a black dress shirt open at the neck was, Margaret decided, sinfully gorgeous. All men were definitely *not* created equal, and Gib was a cut above the Texas herd.

Gib was talking to Alison, who had carried her typewriter to him as soon as he'd entered the house.

Calm down, Margaret, she told herself. But it was there again, that thrumming, pulsing heat low in her body and the vivid images in her mind of making exquisite love with Gib.

She couldn't handle any more of this sensual upheaval. Tonight was *definitely* the last time she would see Gib. She wanted to forget him and the unsettling reactions she had to him, and get on with a life focused on Alison.

"Well," she said, a tad too loudly, "shall we go? I took the car seat out of my car and we'll have to buckle it into yours. I've fed Alison already, so she'll be content, for a while at least, with nibbles of this and that on her high-chair tray at the restaurant.

"Or maybe she won't be happy at all. I really don't know, because this is the first time I've taken her to a…" Margaret stopped speaking and sighed. "I'm babbling."

Gib nodded, a serious expression on his face.

"You certainly are," he said. "Is something wrong, Margaret?"

"No. Yes. You're a very confusing man, Gibson. You're supposedly very angry at me, for what happened when we—" Margaret wiggled one hand in the air "—you know. So why are we going out to dinner if you're mad as blue blazes? This doesn't make the least bit of sense."

Great, Gib thought. That was the last question he wanted to hear Margaret ask him. What should he say? The hell with it...he was going with the truth.

"The truth," he repeated aloud, "is that for reasons I can't explain, I've been unable to get you off my mind, Margaret Madison. You've cast some kind of spell over me that is annoying, to say the least. Why are we going out? So I can get a grip on reality in regard to you, then move on."

"Oh, I see," she said, then lifted her chin. "Thank you. I appreciate your honesty. I might as well tell you that I invited you here for a meal, for exactly the same reason. You're always on my mind, Gibson, and enough is enough."

"You're going out with me so that you can forget about me?"

Margaret nodded. "Yes." She smiled pleasantly. "That's it in a nutshell, and it's exactly why you're going out with me. Shall we be on our way?"

Gib raised one hand. "Now, wait just a—" he glanced quickly at Alison "—darn minute here. I realize you're echoing what I said, but hearing it coming back at me, I don't like the sound of it at all.''

"Why not? Gibson, you said you wanted to get a grip on reality about me. Well, my reality is that I have a toddler, who requires the majority of my time and attention. Alison's existence places me in a world you want no part of, which is perfectly understandable, considering your age.''

"My age? My age!'' Gib yelled. "What, pray tell, is wrong with my age? I'm not that much older than you are, you know. I—''

Alison burst into tears.

"Ah, damn,'' Gib said. "Now I've done it.''

"Do not swear in this home,'' Margaret said, none too quietly. "And don't yell in front of my baby.''

Margaret lifted Alison into her arms, glared at Gibson, then directed her attention to soothing the upset baby.

Gib counted slowly to ten, reining in his temper, which resulted immediately in him feeling horribly guilty about causing Alison to cry.

He was setting records for messing up, he thought. He hadn't been in the house for ten minutes and already he had one of the female residents in tears, and the other one considering strangling him.

"Hey, Alison,'' he said gently, "I'm sorry, kiddo. I didn't mean to scare you.''

He reached out to pat Alison on the back just as Margaret shifted her hold, causing Gib's hand to cover Margaret's on Alison's pinafore. Margaret's head snapped up and her gaze collided with Gib's.

Neither moved, nor hardly breathed.

They simply stood there, looking directly into each other's eyes, their hands as one on Alison's tiny back. The baby stilled, suddenly silent and seemingly content to be held in the protective circle.

Spell weaver, Gib thought rather hazily. Margaret Madison was definitely a spell weaver. He should pull his hand away and step back, break the strange and mystical hold she had cast over him. That was what he *should* do, but he knew he wasn't going to. Not yet.

The sound of her racing heartbeat echoed in Margaret's ears. She was pinned in place by Gib's mesmerizing eyes, unable to tear her gaze from his.

She felt separated from herself, as though observing from afar a Margaret holding her precious child with the added warmth and strength from Gib's hand covering her own.

What a lovely portrait they made, she thought dreamily, from her faraway place. The mother, the father, the trusting and innocent child...perfect. The attractive woman, the handsome man, the cute baby with the funny hair and adorable face...beautiful.

"Kitty," Alison said happily, clapping her hands.

Margaret and Gib both jumped in surprise at the sudden sound. Gib jerked his hand away from Margaret's, took some steps backward and made a major production of examining his watch.

Margaret quickly averted her eyes from Gib, looking instead at Alison and asking the baby if she was all right now, which she obviously was.

"We…" Gib cleared his throat when he heard the gritty sound of his voice. "We should be on our way."

Margaret set Alison on her feet, then sighed.

"Gib, let's forget about going out to dinner, okay?" she said, looking somewhere above his right shoulder. "It seems rather silly, since we've both confessed to why we were going in the first place."

"But—"

"I'm serious, Gibson. I can't explain the effect we have on each other. It may be as simple as basic lust, but eating dinner together isn't going to solve anything. What's needed here is time and distance, not seeing each other at all, and allowing this…whatever it is to dim, then disappear completely."

"But you have to come with me tonight, Margaret," Gib said, hooking one hand on the back of his neck.

"I don't *have* to do anything with you, Gibson McKinley." Margaret nodded. "Yes, I've made up my mind. Alison and I are staying home. You and I should agree to go our separate ways."

Margaret glanced over her shoulder just as Alison headed toward the hallway.

"Whoa, madam," Margaret said, starting across the room. "With the day you've had, I don't want you out of my sight for one second."

Alison squealed in delight as she saw Margaret in pursuit. The toddler picked up speed to go as fast as her little legs would carry her.

"I'm coming to get you," Margaret sang out.

Alone in the living room, Gib indulged himself in muttering several earthy expletives.

Man, what a disaster, he thought. Margaret was now refusing to leave the house with him. There was a surprise baby shower across town with people anticipating the arrival of the guests of honor. Amy Madison Bishop was going to put a contract out on his life if he didn't deliver Margaret and Alison to the party as promised.

And what was this "it may be as simple as basic lust" junk that Margaret was dishing out? She didn't really believe that, did she? *He* certainly didn't, not for a minute.

It shouldn't matter what she thought, considering the fact that they wouldn't be seeing each other after tonight, but it *did* matter, damn it.

Man, he was a complete mess. He sure hadn't liked hearing Margaret parroting his own words as to why she had agreed to have dinner with him. Why was it a perfectly reasonable plan for him, yet felt like a punch in the gut when he learned she wanted a means by which to erase *him* from her thoughts?

There was no doubt about it, this woman was driving him right over the edge of sanity.

Margaret's determination to dust him off was not acceptable. No way. So, okay, he'd been going to do the same thing to her, but he'd changed his mind.

Why?

Was his male ego just working overtime? Was he so accustomed to having women fawning over him that he was royally bent out of shape because one female wanted him to hit the road?

Or was his subconscious conducting some sort of inner inventory? Was it letting him know that his existence was lacking a very special something, a very special someone?

A someone with a *baby?*

No, no, no. He couldn't handle a rerun of all that was yet to come in Alison's life. Margaret Madison might very well be the woman of his dreams. Margaret Madison the mother was not.

So, now what?

Hell, he didn't know.

His subconscious was going to have to sit down and shut up for a while, because the immediate problem was how to get Margaret and Alison to the crummy baby shower.

"I'm sorry I was gone so long," Margaret said, coming back into the room carrying Alison. "We made a diaper pit stop." She settled the baby among the toys on the floor, then went to where Gib was standing. "As I was saying…good night and goodbye, Gibson."

"Margaret, please," Gib said, producing his best one-hundred-watt smile. "Let's be mature adults about this. We both have to eat and I, for one, am starving. Let's go have a pleasant dinner."

"No."

Gib stared up at the ceiling for a long moment, then frowned at Margaret.

"You're being very difficult," he said.

"I certainly am not," she said, planting her hands on her hips. "I'm being realistic. There is no point in our sharing a meal this evening, because we now know the real reason we were going to spend those hours together in the first place."

"I'm rethinking that," Gib said, "but there isn't time to get into it now." He threw up his hands. "I've blown it. Oh, man, have I blown it."

"What are you talking about?"

"Margaret, you must come with me, because Amy is having a surprise baby shower for you and Alison at Tux and Nancy Bishop's house tonight."

Margaret's eyes widened. "What?"

"It's true, I swear it is. Smug jerk that I am, I told Amy I could get you there at the proper time."

"But I don't want a baby shower," Margaret said, splaying one hand on her chest.

"Amy figured that would be what you'd say, but all of your friends were determined to do this. That's why it had to be a surprise. Please, Margaret, don't ruin this for Amy. She has worked so hard to pull this off. It's not her fault I blew it. Think of Amy's feelings at the moment, not your own."

"Oh, dear. I wouldn't intentionally upset Amy for the world, but—"

"Of course you wouldn't. We have to go, or we'll be late."

Margaret sighed. "Yes, all right." She paused. "How on earth am I going to act surprised now that I know about the shower?"

"Fake it."

"Drat. Well, I'll get Alison's diaper bag. You carry the car seat."

"Got it."

"Wait a minute, Gibson. What did you mean when you said you were 'rethinking' our mutual goal to forget about each other?"

"Exactly that...I'm rethinking it. I'm beginning to believe that we should discover exactly what this is that's happening between us before we just erase it from our lives."

"You're out of your mind."

"That, lovely Margaret," Gib said wearily, "is a fact that I'm starting to realize I'll have to accept as being sadly true."

Chapter Nine

As she, Gib and Alison drove away from the house, Margaret wished that she could stamp her feet and throw a tantrum the way Alison did when a situation didn't satisfy her.

She knew the baby shower was being given out of love from Amy, and genuine caring and friendship from those attending. But she simply didn't like being the center of attention.

There were times, she supposed, when a person had to put aside their own likes and dislikes to protect the feelings of others. This was definitely one of those occasions.

Margaret looked at the back seat where Alison was babbling to herself and pointing to whatever caught her fancy beyond the window as they whizzed past.

As she redirected her attention to the road, Margaret slid a quick glance at Gib as he maneuvered the expensive automobile through the busy traffic.

Gibson McKinley was a very complicated and confusing man, Margaret thought. He'd arrived at her house and soon divulged that he wished to spend the evening with her to erase her from his mind.

Before he left the house, he'd declared that he was rethinking that goal and now thought they should discover exactly what was happening between them.

When she'd told him he was crazy, he'd readily agreed that he was, indeed, out of his mind!

So, now what? The ball was in her court.

Gib was making overtures to continue seeing her. That, however, did not mean she had to comply.

Margaret looked at Gib again, allowing her gaze to linger, drinking in the sight of his strong but gentle hands on the steering wheel, his wide shoulders, his muscled thighs clearly defined beneath the material of his slacks.

The now-familiar heat began to swirl through her, causing her breasts to feel heavy, aching for Gib's soothing touch. The fire swept lower, coiling, pulsing in the darkness of her femininity.

Oh, how she wanted this man. Just looking at him made her passion soar. Remembering the ecstasy of making love with him caused her to go up in flames of desire.

But it wasn't just lust.

She'd tossed out that sassy statement while not believing it for a second. Emotions were involved, as well. She *liked* Gibson McKinley as a person, a man. He was intelligent, ambitious, charming, caring and kind.

She'd heard endless glowing accounts from her daughter for many months before actually meeting the owner of *The Houston Holler* at Amy and Blue's wedding.

The reception had been the first Cinderella night with Gib, Margaret thought, shifting her gaze to the side window. The evening had had a romantic aura to it, due to witnessing the exchanging of forever vows between her happy daughter and new son-in-law.

And she, Margaret Madison, had danced the night away beneath the Texas stars in the arms of an incredibly handsome and virile man.

And savored the memories.

On the second Cinderella night she'd been in a strange frame of mind, which had led to lovemaking with Gibson that had been beyond description in its wondrous beauty.

But despite the magical encounters with Gib, there was a part of it all that was grounded in reality, revealing the values and basic goodness of the man himself.

And that, Margaret thought, was possibly more dangerous to her orderly world than her physical attraction to Gib. That she liked, respected and, yes, trusted Gib was the stuff of which a foundation of friendship could be built, a friendship that, if properly nurtured, might very well lead to love.

Margaret shook her head.

Dear heaven, no. She would not—could not—fall in love with Gibson. She would be guaranteeing herself a gigantic serving of heartache, because Gib was not about to become seriously involved with a woman who had a baby. No, there was no possibility of love on the horizon in regard to Gib.

So then why did Gib want to *discover* what they might have together, when he knew Alison was on the scene? Did he have moments when he forgot that Alison existed?

Margaret smiled.

If Gib witnessed a day like the one Alison had just dished up for her mommy, the toddler's presence would be etched indelibly in Gib's mind.

Oh, dear, Margaret thought, she was mentally rambling, and not reaching any concrete decisions as to what to do regarding seeing Gib again. Why couldn't she hold fast to her decision to forget him, darn it? She was being so wishy-washy it was disgusting.

They were within two blocks of Tux and Nancy's house, she realized. She'd better put her confusing thoughts on hold and concentrate on determining how a person acted surprised when they weren't.

"Wow," Margaret said. "Oh, my, oh, wow."

Gib glanced over at her. "Pardon me?"

"I'm practicing being surprised. Did I sound absolutely thrilled?"

"No," he said, laughing. "You sounded more like someone who just found a big wad of bubblegum on the bottom of her shoe."

"Drat. How's this?" Margaret paused. "My goodness, what a surprise. I'm so very…" She moaned. "Just forget it. I'm going with surprised to the point of being speechless."

"Excellent idea," Gib said, still smiling. "You don't do phony well at all." His smile faded. "Which is just one of the things I admire about you, Margaret. You're very real."

"Thank you, but I wasn't being the *real* me the night we… Never mind. This isn't the time or place to discuss that."

"No, it isn't, except I'd like to say that since I've gotten to know you better, I have a greater understanding of your mind-set that night."

"You do?" Margaret said, her eyes widening slightly.

Gib nodded. "It's the same type of thing as a bachelor party, for example. The husband-to-be's behavior is not only accepted, it has become a tradition for him to go off the deep end."

"I wouldn't call making love with you as going off the deep end," Margaret said, laughing.

"You know what I mean." Gib paused. "What I'm trying to say here, Margaret, is that I apologize for my harsh words about what happened. You weren't using me, you were simply freeing yourself of self-imposed restraints for one night of your life."

"Yes, that's exactly right."

"Once I got my overblown ego out of the way, I've been able to view things much more clearly. I'm sincerely sorry for my behavior, and I hope you'll accept my apology.''

''Yes. Yes, of course I do, and I thank you very much, Gib. I—''

''We have arrived.''

Margaret forced herself to push aside her shock at Gib's sudden apology and to ignore the warm, fuzzy feeling his sincere words were causing to hum through her. She glanced out the window.

''Oh, my gosh,'' she said. ''Look at all the cars. This is getting worse by the minute.''

Gib pulled in to the driveway of the house and turned off the ignition.

''Okay, here's the plan. You've seen all the vehicles and I've said something brilliant like there must be a party being held on the block. We're on our way to dinner, but have stopped here so that I can pick up an article from Amy, because she and Blue are in town to spend the evening with Tux and Nancy.''

''How clever,'' Margaret said dryly.

''Leave Alison's diaper bag in the car for now. We wouldn't take it in for a five-minute deal. I'll come back out later and get it. We'll go into the backyard, because that's where the two couples are enjoying the lovely Houston evening.''

''Oh-h-h,'' Margaret said, rolling her eyes. ''I want to go home.''

''Up,'' Alison said, wiggling in the car seat. ''Up, up, up.''

''Yes, ma'am,'' Gib said, looking back and smiling at her. "Your wish is my command, Texas baby. Just remember to keep that aversion to parked cars when you become a teenager."

"No, no, no," Alison said, shaking her head.

Gib laughed and got out of the car. Margaret unsnapped her seat belt and opened the door as Gib came around the vehicle. He lifted Alison from the seat and settled her into the crook of his arm. The baby clapped her hands. Margaret closed the door and extended her arms to her daughter, but Alison turned farther into Gib, wrapping her little hands around his neck.

"Come to Mommy, Alison," Margaret said.

"No, no, no," the baby said.

"I'll carry her," Gib said. "We're buddies. Right, kiddo?"

"Kid-dough," Alison said. "Dough. Dough."

"But…" Margaret stopped speaking and frowned. "What I mean is, we'll look like a… Oh, never mind."

"A family?" Gib said, raising his eyebrows. "Margaret, tongues are going to wag over our being together, whether I'm carrying Alison or not. Do you really care what people think?"

"No."

"Then let's go, before that yardful of people pop a seam trying to keep quiet."

Margaret threw up her hands in defeat and started toward the rear of Tux and Nancy's house.

Class, Gib thought two hours later. He had used that word early on to describe Margaret Madison, and it certainly applied tonight. She'd done her stunned-speechless performance, blushed prettily, then smiled at everyone gathered in her honor.

She'd opened the gifts with Alison's help, thanked each person graciously and allowed Alison to shred the gift wrapping to her heart's delight.

Gib swept his gaze over the yard, nodding in approval at the sparkling fairy lights that cast a festive glow as darkness fell. People were chatting as they sat in lawn chairs, enjoying servings of delicious cake, ice cream and punch.

Blue caught Gib's eye and waved him over to join him and his brothers. Greetings were exchanged between the four men, and Blue congratulated Gib on delivering Margaret and Alison to the shower at exactly the right moment.

"Amy is so tickled that her mother was genuinely surprised," Blue said. "Amy will probably write her next article for free, Gib. Cancel that. Give her a raise. Anyway, you're the hero of the night. Surprise parties are not easy to pull off."

"No joke," Gib said dryly.

"Did you see that neat push toy Alison got?" Tux said. "It makes noise and pops up little balls when she moves it. They sure have different stuff these days from when we were kids. I'm sure going to enjoy playing with our baby's toys."

"You'll be too tired to play with toys," Bram said. "You have to take your shifts of bottles and diapers. And burping. Don't forget burping."

"I intend to do my part," Tux said, nodding. "And I'm looking forward to it. I can hardly wait for our baby to be born. It sure seems like a long time between now and Christmas, when Nancy's due."

"You're getting the ultimate Christmas present this year, Tux," Blue said. "Man, I hope I become a father in the not-too-distant future."

"Me, too," Bram added. "The house that Glory and I are designing is going to have room for oodles of kids."

"That's good," Gib said. "Alison will eventually have lots of friends to play with. That social interaction is important, you know. She'll be older than your children, but she still..." He stopped speaking as he realized all three Bishops were looking at him intently. "What? Do I have cake on my chin, or something?"

"No-o-o," Tux said. "It's just that for a moment there you sure sounded like Alison's father. You know, being concerned about...What did you call it?...her social interaction."

Gib shifted uncomfortably in his chair. "I was just adding to the conversation."

"You certainly looked natural carrying Alison into the yard earlier," Blue said.

"Well, I do have a grown daughter, you know," Gib retorted. "I have experience with little kids."

"Alison sure is cute," Tux said, still directing his full attention to Gib.

"Yes, she is," Gib agreed. "Her funny hair just

makes her even cuter. She's smart as a tack, too, really bright. Margaret reads to her every day, which is great. She's a fantastic mother. I think she's... Would you guys knock it off? You're all staring at me again."

"Gib," Blue said, smiling, "if you marry Margaret I think you'd be my stepfather-in-law. How's that for a title?"

"Whoa," Gib said, holding up one hand. "Who said anything about marriage? We're talking about Alison, remember?"

"And Alison's mother," Bram said. "Gibson, my man, you've got all the signs of a guy going down for the count. Margaret Madison McKinley. Now, that has a very nice ring to it."

"You're crazy," Gib said, scowling.

"It's true that Bram is a card short of a deck," Tux said. "But in this case I'd say he's right."

"Yep," Blue agreed.

"Well, damn," Tux said. "You'll have a neat new kid before I get mine, Gib."

"Now, look—"

At that exact moment Alison appeared and flung herself across Gib's knees.

"Up," she said.

Gib lifted her onto his lap and the toddler snuggled closer, sticking her thumb into her mouth.

"Are you all partied out, kiddo?" Gib said, ruffling Alison's hair.

He looked up to see Blue, Bram and Tux grinning at him.

"You're dead wrong," Gib said, glaring at the trio. "I never intend to marry again, and I sure wouldn't sign up to start over raising a baby. No way."

"Kitty," Alison said sleepily without removing her thumb from her mouth. "Da-da."

The Bishop boys whooped with laughter.

Just before ten o'clock that night Margaret came back into the living room after putting Alison to bed. Gib was placing the last of the shower presents on a chair.

"So many lovely gifts," Margaret said. "I feel rather…oh, I don't know…guilty, I think."

Gib straightened and turned to look at her.

"Whatever for?" he said.

"Alison has more clothes and toys than one child could ever need, and there are so many children in the world who have nothing."

Gib closed the distance between them and gripped Margaret lightly by the shoulders.

"Enough of that kind of talk," he said. "Alison was among those who had very little until you came along. She deserves those gifts, and so do you."

"Well, the least I can do is take what she outgrows over to the foster home where she was staying. I'm sure that Maggie can put them to good use in her stash, as she calls it."

"That's an excellent idea," Gib said, not releasing his hold on her.

"Would you like some coffee and a sandwich,

Gib? We didn't have any dinner, and I imagine you're starving. The cake and punch were delicious, but it wasn't exactly a hearty meal.''

"A sandwich sounds great."

Margaret laughed. "It will be your reward for suffering through a baby shower."

"I had a nice time, I truly did. Your family and friends are terrific people." Gib chuckled. "Those Bishop boys are really something when they all get together."

"I noticed that you spent most of the evening with them. They're wonderful young men. Amy is so happy with Blue. I enjoyed chatting with Jana-John and Abe Bishop, too." Margaret paused. "So! Let's go see what fixings I have in the refrigerator to make sandwiches."

"In a minute."

Gib brushed his lips over Margaret's in a featherlike caress that caused a shiver to whisper down her spine. Then his mouth melted over hers, his tongue parting her lips to slip into the sweet darkness beyond.

Margaret wrapped her arms around Gib's neck, inching her fingers into his thick hair and urging his mouth harder onto hers. She savored the feel of Gib, the taste of his mouth, his aroma of woodsy aftershave and soap.

Gib lifted his head to draw a sharp breath, then slanted the kiss in the other direction.

The room cluttered with gifts disappeared into a hazy mist of passion that was soaring higher, hotter, swirling as it carried them further and further away from reality.

There were only the two of them, the want, the need, the incredible heat.

No. A little voice spoke in Margaret's mind. She mustn't do this. No matter how much she wanted to make love with Gibson McKinley, to experience again the ecstasy of joining her body with his, she must not do this.

Margaret broke the kiss, then shifted her hands to splay on Gib's chest. She stepped backward, forcing him to release her as she wrapped her hands around her elbows.

"No," she said, hearing the thread of breathlessness in her voice. "This isn't going to happen. I'm not going to make love with you, Gib."

Gib willed his aroused body back under control, struggled for command over the ache of need, the burning want, of Margaret.

"Why not?" he said, his voice gritty. "You want me, Margaret, every bit as much as I want you. Can you deny that?"

Margaret shook her head.

"Then why are you doing this to us?" he said, his voice rising.

Margaret swept one hand through the air. "Look around this room, Gibson. Those gifts are for a baby." She placed a hand on her heart. "*My* baby. Alison is real. She's sleeping in her crib down the hall. This isn't a last fling before she arrives. She's here!"

"And that means you're no longer a woman?" he said, planting his hands on his hips. "You no longer have wants, needs of a normal, healthy woman? Did you shut down your femininity when you became Alison's mother?"

"No, of course not, but I have to behave in a responsible manner. I don't sleep with a man on a whim, Gib. It has to be special, important, part of a growing relationship that is being nurtured. There's no room in my life for that, and especially not with a man who wants no part of raising a child."

Gib raked one hand through his hair. "Damn it, Margaret, why can't you separate the two things? Why can't we enjoy each other, the pleasure we bring to each other, and view it as something far removed from your existence with Alison?"

"No," she said, shaking her head. "Alison is part of who I am as a woman. Can't you understand that? She is a part of the essence of me, the person. You can't have the parts of me that suit your needs and ignore the rest. It doesn't work that way, Gib."

Gib took a deep breath and let it out slowly, reining in his growing frustration and the sharp edge of anger beginning to creep over him.

"Margaret," he said quietly, "I like Alison, you know I do. I enjoy being with her, watching her discover new things, seeing the awe, the wonder, on her face. She brings back cherished memories of when Betsy was small, of viewing my daughter as a miracle, like a flower opening its petals, one by one."

Unexpected and unwelcome tears stung Margaret's eyes as she listened to Gib's gently spoken words. She fought against the threatening tears, and was determined not to succumb to the amalgam of emotions assaulting her.

"No, I don't intend to remarry," Gib went on, "nor do I wish to commit myself to fatherhood all over again. But I *do* want to be a special and important part of your life, Margaret Madison. And I *do* want to spend time with your daughter. For how long? I don't know. But if we both understand that, no one will get hurt."

"Except Alison," Margaret whispered, still fighting against her tears.

"What?"

Margaret began to roam around the cluttered room, picking up a toy, putting it back down, touching one thing, then another, as she attempted to create a semblance of order out of the chaos in her mind.

"Suppose," she said, continuing her trek, "just suppose I could become comfortable with your proposed plan. We spend time together, sleep together, I presume, have a commitment of sorts for...what?...weeks, months? Then for whatever reason, we agree to end it, go our separate ways, and that is that."

Margaret stopped and picked up a teddy bear, smoothing the soft brown fur with one fingertip. She wrapped both hands around the toy and tucked it beneath her chin, only then meeting Gib's gaze.

"At that point, Gib," she said, "what happens to Alison? You would have been a major part of her life during the time we were together, then suddenly you'd be gone. She'd miss you, would be looking for you, waiting for you. She'd suffer the pain of losing someone important in her world, just as a child of a divorce does. I won't put my daughter through that by selfishly indulging in an…an affair."

Gib frowned. "I don't think Alison would react that way. There will be men in her life that come and go, like Tux, Blue and Bram."

"Who will *stay* in her life."

"Alison is just a baby, Margaret. She'd forget about me in a blink of an eye. It would be out of sight, out of mind."

And what about Alison's mother? Margaret thought. How long would it take *her* to forget Gibson McKinley? What if she fell in love with him, then had to watch him walk away, taking her heart with him? He was already consuming her thoughts more often than she cared to admit. To even be entertaining the idea of having an affair with Gib was foolish, dangerous and potentially heartbreaking.

An affair. Dear Lord, what a sordid-sounding word. How tacky and cheap.

"No," Margaret said, nestling the bear back into its tissue-paper bed before straightening to look at Gib. "I am not affair material, Gibson. It's not who I am. I had my out-of-character fling with you before Alison arrived in my home. I won't do that again. I have to be true to who I am, or I'll lose my inner peace."

Gib narrowed his eyes. "Exactly what is it that you're saying?"

"That we're on different wavelengths. That doesn't make one of us wrong, the other right. It simply means we aren't compatible in our thinking and...that we shouldn't see each other again."

"Oh? And what about the strange force that continually pulls us together? Don't you want to know what that is, what it means?"

"For what purpose? To justify sleeping with you because, yes, there is a tremendous attraction between us? What if it's love, Gib? What if we discover we've fallen in love with each other? Wouldn't that be a dandy mess?"

"That wouldn't happen," he said, his voice rising. "My God, Margaret, we're mature adults, not starry-eyed teenagers. Love has to be nurtured, gently, carefully allowed to grow. It doesn't hit you between the eyes when you aren't looking, like in the movies and romance novels."

"Is that a fact? Then why your desire to *discover* what is happening between us? If it isn't the seedling of love, then why don't you know what it is?"

Gib ran his hand over the back of his neck.

"You're making this much too complicated," he said, frowning. "I simply believe we might discover something deeper, richer than the average—"

"Affair?"

"Yes, affair! That, to me, is not a nasty word. It's a mature understanding of the boundaries of a relationship. It does not include falling in love, because love doesn't happen unless you want it to. You have to work at it.''

Margaret sighed. ''Gib, we're just going around in circles. I'm tired and I have to get these gifts put away before Alison dives into them in the morning. I know I said we'd have a sandwich, but I'm going to be a terrible hostess and withdraw my offer.''

''We haven't found a solution to our problem,'' Gib said.

''There isn't one.''

''We don't know that. Look, why don't we go to the family restaurant we were supposedly eating at tonight? We'll take Alison, then talk about this some more after she goes to bed. Tomorrow night?''

''I don't see any point in it. We're poles apart in our views.''

''One more chance. If we don't reach a workable solution tomorrow evening, then that's that. Please, Margaret?''

''I just don't—''

''Please?''

''Oh, all right.''

''Good. That's good. I'll pick you and Alison up at six o'clock.''

''Five o'clock. I'm going to attempt to feed Alison at the restaurant.''

Gib nodded, then crossed the room to stand in front of Margaret. He framed her face in his hands and kissed her lightly.

''Thank you. Good night, Margaret.''

''Good night, Gib.''

Margaret watched Gib leave the house, then went to the door to lock it. She returned to the array of gifts and picked up the teddy bear.

"Oh, bear," she said to the toy, "what on earth am I doing?"

Chapter Ten

The next evening it took Margaret more time than
usual to settle Alison down for bed, after the baby's
big night on the town. When Margaret finally returned to the living room, Gib was sitting on the sofa
and grinning.

"Don't start again," she said, smiling. "Don't you
dare start laughing again, Gibson McKinley. I'm a
breath away from getting the hiccups as it is." She
sank onto a chair and pressed her hands flat on her
stomach. "Oh, good heavens."

"I'm under control." Gib chuckled. "It's just that
every time I picture Alison throwing that cherry tomato, I fall apart. I'm telling you, Margaret, she's
destined to be on the women's Olympic basketball
dream team. She whizzed that tomato over to the

next table and right into that guy's cup of coffee. Two points. No, that was definitely a three-point shot.''

"Stop," Margaret said, laughing. "Don't talk about it. It was terrible, embarrassing and...one of the funniest things I've ever seen. You do realize, don't you, that we can never go back to that restaurant?''

"No joke. We're banned from that place for life." Gib leaned his head back on the top of the sofa and took a deep breath. "Lord, this feels good.''

"What does?''

He lifted his head again and met Margaret's merry gaze.

"I can't remember when I've laughed so much, or been so thoroughly tickled by something," he said. "This whole evening has been wonderful. I wouldn't have missed it for the world.''

"Well, it was educational, to say the least. Alison is not quite ready for restaurant dining.''

Their smiles slowly faded as they continued to look directly into each other's eyes.

Margaret tore her gaze from Gib's and stared at her hands clutched tightly in her lap.

"No," she whispered. "Don't, Gib, just don't.''

Gib leaned forward, resting his elbows on his knees and lacing his fingers loosely together.

"Margaret," he said, "we have to talk about this.''

She shook her head.

"Look at me," he said. "Please.''

Margaret sighed as she lifted her head again.

"We shared something special with Alison this evening. A memory was created that was funny...and ours. What happened in that restaurant is the type of thing you later say, 'Remember the time...'"

"What point are you trying to make, Gib?"

"The point is, we can't erase anything that has taken place between us. As we address the future, the past we've shared can't be ignored. We have our memories. We have memories of being with Alison, too. All those memories are rich, real, treasures to keep. I don't want to walk out of your life, Margaret, or out of Alison's. You're both very important to me."

"For as long as it lasts," Margaret said.

"Yes."

"No. I won't do that to Alison." Margaret lifted her chin. "In fact, I won't put *myself* in the path of possible heartbreak. You feel that people can't fall in love if they make up their minds not to. Well, color me a romantic, but I believe that the heart has a stronger voice than the mind when it comes to love. I will *not* run the risk of falling in love with you. I have no intention of making love with you again, Gibson."

Gib got to his feet and wandered aimlessly around the room.

"I see," he said finally, coming to a halt next to Margaret's chair.

"Do you?" she said, looking up at him. "There's nothing here for you, Gib."

Gib narrowed his eyes. "You think that all I want is to get you into bed again? Thanks a hell of a lot, Margaret."

"I'm not condemning you for it, Gib. We're mature adults who are extremely attracted to each other. It stands to reason that making love would be a part of our relationship. If we had one. Which we don't."

"I'll have you know that being with you brings more than just sex into my life."

"All right, I'll give you that. However, the lack of sex would create a glaring void. Chaste little kisses at the door are not your style, Mr. McKinley."

"You, Mrs. Madison," he said, pointing a finger at her, "are making me angry. I am *not* a sex maniac."

"No, you're a healthy, normal man. I'm a healthy, normal woman, too, Gib, but I chose my life-style when I made the decision to adopt Alison. That existence does not include having an affair, and possibly having to deal with the pain of a broken heart somewhere down the road."

Gib took a deep breath and let it out slowly, puffing his cheeks in the process.

"Okay," he said. "Try this. You said that Blue, Bram and Tux would be in and out of Alison's life."

"Yes, they will. Everyone is busy, but Alison will get to know them, see them when possible, have them as male influences."

"Well, why can't you add me to that list?"

"Whatever for?"

"Because I laughed right out loud tonight," Gib said, none too quietly. "Because I had fun, pure and simple. Because I'm capable of being around you without trying to seduce you, for crying out loud."

"Shh, you'll wake up Alison."

"Well, cripe, you make me sound like a jerk who is ruled by testosterone."

"So what are you suggesting? That we back up here and become friends? Not lovers, just friends?"

"Yes," Gib said slowly. "Yes, I think that's what I'm saying."

"You *think?*"

"All I know is, I don't want to be deprived of your company, or Alison's, either. So your ground rules are no making love again. I can live with that, despite your low opinion of me on the subject. I'll just be in the picture like the Bishop boys. It wouldn't be often enough to upset Alison if I..."

"Disappeared forever?" Margaret finished for him.

"Yes. I don't know how I'll feel about this arrangement in the future, but the way it's set up now, no one can get hurt."

"I hope you realize," Margaret said, frowning, "that *I* may have a negative opinion to express about this arrangement in the future, as well."

"My dear Margaret," Gib said, smiling, "it would never occur to me that you wouldn't air your views on any subject we're discussing. That's a compliment, by the way."

Margaret laughed. "Are you sure?"

Gib reached down, grasped one of Margaret's hands and urged her upward. She complied and Gib encircled her waist with his arms. Margaret rested her hands lightly on his shoulders.

"Are you willing to try my plan?" Gib said.

"Yes, all right."

"Then I'll call you in a week or so."

A flicker of disappointment nudged Margaret.

A week or so? she mentally repeated. It would be that long before she heard from Gib again? Fine, that was fine. It was for the best, really. They were going to be friends who saw each other occasionally. This arrangement was much better for both Alison's *and* her emotional well-being. Oh, why did she continually have to have this argument with herself to keep on the proper emotional track?

"I guess I'll be on my way," Gib said, not moving.

"Thank you for dinner."

"You're welcome," he said, smiling. "And three cheers for little girls and cherry tomatoes. They are the stuff of which memories are made."

"Indeed," she said, matching his smile.

Their grins faded, then Gib brushed his lips over Margaret's in a featherlike caress. In the next instant he captured her mouth in a searing kiss, parting her lips, meeting her tongue in a rhythmic duel.

Gib pulled Margaret closer, nestling her to his aroused body. She entwined her arms around his neck. The kiss deepened and passions soared. Heat licked through them with hot, burning flames of want and need. Heartbeats thundered, and their breathing became labored, echoing in the quiet room.

Slowly, reluctantly, Gib ended the kiss, then eased Margaret away from him.

"You were right," he said, his voice raspy.

"Hmm?" Margaret said dreamily.

"I'm not cut out for chaste little kisses by the door, but I'll work on that. Good night, Margaret."

As Gib left the house, Margaret sank quickly onto the chair, realizing her legs were trembling. She placed one hand on her racing heart, willing it to return to a normal tempo.

She and Gibson McKinley were going to be just friends? she thought. Who were they kidding?

She slipped off her shoes and wiggled her toes in the plush carpeting.

Just friends. All right, so be it. If Gib could handle it, so could she. They were, after all, mature adults, not randy teenagers. They'd see each other on occasion, enjoy the outing, and that would be that. And Alison would certainly benefit from the male influence Gib would provide.

But Gib wasn't even going to call for a week or so?

"Oh, Margaret, shut up," she said aloud. "You're getting crazy again."

Gib entered his office, sat down in the soft leather chair, then flipped the page on his desktop calendar.

It was only Wednesday? This week was dragging

by so slowly, it was a crime. He'd told Margaret he'd call her in a week or so. Well, forget the "or so." He was having a ridiculously difficult time waiting out the week.

He leaned back and rubbed his face.

Lord, he was tired. He hadn't slept well for several nights and was thoroughly exhausted. He had not, in fact, had a decent night's sleep since leaving Margaret's home on Sunday evening.

When he did manage to doze, he was plagued by a strange mixture of dreams.

Some were sensuous encounters with Margaret that caused him to awaken bathed in sweat.

Others were whimsical images. One had been Margaret and Alison joining him in flying a kite while balancing on clouds in the sky. Another had been a romp through a sea of cherry tomatoes with Margaret and the baby.

But always present, every time, was Margaret Madison.

He sighed.

He had been the idiot who'd proposed that they agree to be only friends. It had been his last-ditch effort to keep her from refusing to see him ever again.

Why was he doing this? He didn't want a serious relationship with anyone, let alone with a woman with a baby, despite what those cocky Bishop boys had decided. So why was he hanging on by his fingertips, trying to stay as close as possible to Margaret?

Hell, he didn't know. All he was certain of was that he had no intention of being shown the door at Margaret's until *he* was ready to walk through it.

No wonder he and Alison got along so well, he thought dryly. He sounded like a little kid hardly older than she was, who was throwing a tantrum.

You can't send me away, Margaret Madison, until I've decided I want to go. So there!

Cripe, he was in the middle of a second childhood at fifty years old. Was that what happened when you hit the half-century mark?

Gib glared at the calendar again.

Saturday was the day. The birthday that was turning him into a loony. The big five-oh. He'd had a practice run at it last night at Betsy's, with cake and ice cream, since the family was going out of town for a week. They'd given him an ivory checker set as a birthday gift.

Checkers? Gib mused. Was that a subtle message? Were Betsy and company acknowledging his teetering years by giving him the game that was played by old men in rocking chairs on front porches?

Ah, damn, why couldn't he shut off his mind for a while?

If he wasn't thinking about Margaret, the subject matter was his age, or Alison, then right back to center on Margaret.

Enough, already.

Gib snatched up the receiver to the telephone.

He'd told Margaret he would call her in a week or so. Well, he was bending that statement a bit. He'd phone now to hopefully make plans for Saturday, which would only be a day shy of a week since he'd seen her.

He'd survive his fiftieth birthday by ignoring it. He'd concentrate on a nice outing with Margaret and Alison, and the glum event of turning fifty would be over at dawn's light on Sunday.

Gib nodded decisively and punched in the memorized numbers on the receiver.

The telephone rang as Margaret was wiping off Alison's high-chair tray after breakfast. The toddler was sitting on the floor, happily beating on a pan with a wooden spoon. Margaret lifted the receiver on the wall telephone.

"Hello?"

"Good morning, Margaret. I hope I'm not disturbing you."

A warm flutter slithered down Margaret's spine as she heard the rich, deep timbre of Gib's voice. She was smiling, she knew it, and decided it didn't matter, since Gibson wasn't capable of seeing through the wires of a telephone.

"No, you're not disturbing me." Margaret laughed. "I'm being serenaded by the resident rock-and-roll drummer."

"I can hear the music, although I don't recognize the song."

"It's known only to the composer," Margaret said. "Is something wrong, Gib? I didn't expect to hear from you so soon."

"No, no, all is well. I...um...just thought it best to call and see if we could get together on Saturday, before you made other plans. There's a petting zoo being set up in the parking lot of a mall near my house that I think Alison would enjoy."

"That sounds like fun." Margaret paused. "Oh, dear, I've made arrangements to take some clothes and toys to Maggie's, the foster mother where Alison was staying."

"We could do that first."

"All right. Alison has been taking a late-morning nap these days. I told Maggie I'd be there about one-thirty."

"If I picked you up at one, would that do it?"

"Perfect."

"Great. Have a good week and give Alison a tickle for me."

"Thank you, Gib. Goodbye."

"I'm looking forward to seeing you and Alison. Goodbye, Margaret."

Margaret replaced the receiver slowly, then turned to smile at the little drummer girl.

"We're going to a petting zoo with Gib on Saturday, sweetheart. You know, Gib. He calls you Texas baby and kiddo."

"Dough...dough...dough," Alison yelled, banging the spoon on the pan.

Margaret laughed and resumed her cleaning, making no attempt to curb her smile.

Gib stared at the telephone long after he'd replaced the receiver.

A man named Brian poked his head into the office.

"Hey, boss," he said, "have you got a thing for your phone? I've never seen anyone smiling at a telephone before."

Gib's head snapped up. "I was smiling?"

"Yep. Must have been someone special on the line before you hung up, huh? See ya. I've got a date with a bagel that's waiting for me on my desk."

As Brian disappeared from view, Gib looked at the telephone again.

Someone special? Yes, she was that. Margaret Madison was, indeed, a very special woman. And he'd meant what he'd said. He really was looking forward to seeing Margaret and Alison on Saturday.

Not realizing he was humming a peppy tune, Gib redirected his attention to the stack of papers on his desk and got to work.

There was a lovely breeze accompanying the hot and humid weather on Saturday, making it a perfect day to be outside.

Alison had been so angelic since opening her big blue eyes at dawn that Margaret finally smiled and asked the baby what the con was. Alison threw her arms around Margaret's knees and hugged her, causing Margaret to burst into laughter and get motherly tears in her eyes at the same time.

While Alison was taking her late-morning nap, Margaret followed her usual routine of treating herself to a cup of tea in the peaceful kitchen.

As she wrapped her hands around the warm mug,

she allowed her thoughts to float free, realizing she was not surprised when they centered on the outing that afternoon with Gib.

A soft smile formed on her lips as she remembered the morning hours with Alison. It was as though the toddler knew of the special event planned for the afternoon and was on her best behavior because of it.

I understand, Alison, Margaret thought, because she, too, was eagerly looking forward to the trip to the petting zoo with Gib.

Margaret took a sip of tea and frowned.

To be perfectly honest, she was filled with a sense of anticipation about seeing Gib, the petting zoo being an added bonus.

There was no denying the fact that she'd thought often of Gib since the last time they'd been together. She'd given up trying to push away the images of him in her mind. They refused to budge.

Her *friend* Gib, Margaret reminded herself firmly. They were now, by mutual agreement, only friends, not even considering being lovers.

Could people really do that? Back up a relationship, complete with different rules? Well, by the time the Texas sun had set that night, she'd know the answer to that question.

"Turn right at the next corner," Margaret said, "then go two blocks and turn left."

"Yep," Gib responded.

"Yep," Alison echoed from her car seat in the rear of Gib's vehicle.

"Is there a parrot in this car?" Gib said, laughing. "Or is that my Texas baby I hear?"

"Kitty," Alison yelled, clapping her hands. "Da-da. Kitty."

My Texas baby? Margaret thought, looking quickly over at Gib. As in *his?* No, she was being foolish. It was just a figure of speech. She'd heard Tux say, "How's my girl?" to Alison at the baby shower. It was a manner of speaking that people used all the time.

There was no reason for her heart to have skipped a beat upon hearing Gib say *my* Texas baby. There was no call for the instant warmth that had suffused her as Gib's words swept over her.

Quit being a dumb-dumb, she bluntly admonished herself.

"It's that white house with blue trim on the right there," Margaret said.

"Okay," Gib answered.

"'Kay," Alison repeated. "'Kay. 'Kay."

"I repeat my earlier vow," Gib said, smiling. "I will *never* swear in front of that child."

Gib parked in the driveway of Maggie's house. Margaret carried Alison, while Gib toted the two boxes of clothes and toys for the foster mother's "stash." On the porch Margaret rang the doorbell and heard Maggie sing out a cheerful "I'm coming. Just a minute." Then the door was opened and a smiling Maggie greeted them with a tiny baby tucked in the crook of one arm.

Gib hardly remembered entering the house, acknowledging the introductions and setting the boxes on the floor. All he could focus on was the baby boy Maggie had called Benjamin.

Benjamin, Gib's mind hammered. Ben. It was a good, strong name.

He had coal black hair, big dark eyes and a serious expression on his face as he riveted his gaze on Gib. His little fists were tucked beneath his chin, as though he was ready to take a poke at anyone who messed with him without his permission.

"Sit down, sit down," Maggie said, snapping Gib back to attention. "Oh, Margaret, I can't get over how much Alison has grown in such a short time. She's wonderful."

"Definitely," Margaret said, smiling as they all settled onto the sofa. "How's Benjamin doing?"

"He's coming along remarkably well," Maggie said. "The doctor determined that there wasn't as much drug use by his birth mother as we first feared. Benjamin is sensitive to loud noises and is a restless sleeper, but beyond that he's thriving."

"May I hold him?" Gib heard himself ask.

"Sure," Maggie said.

Margaret looked at Gib in surprise as he nestled the baby boy in his arms.

Dear heaven, she thought, they could be father and son. Benjamin had the same coloring as Gib, and the baby was staring at Gibson as though gazing at a familiar face.

"Hello, Benny," Gib said quietly. "You started life with a rough trip, huh? Well, you're going to be fine. You're a fighter, I can tell."

Alison wiggled off of Margaret's lap and leaned against Gib's knee, raising her arms.

"Up," the toddler said. "Up."

"Oh, we are a tad jealous, are we?" Maggie said, laughing.

Gib scooped Alison onto one thigh.

"See the baby, kiddo?" Gib said to Alison.

"Bee-bee," Alison said, nodding. She touched Benjamin's sleeper-clad foot with one finger. "Bee-bee."

"That's right," Gib said. "Benny is a very special boy, just like you're a very special girl." He looked at Maggie. "What's going to happen to Benny?"

"There will be a court hearing in a month or so," Maggie said. "There's no way to be certain at this point, but it appears that his birth mother will be sentenced to a jail term. She'll probably lose permanent custody of the baby, because she has a long arrest record of drug use and other offenses. The outcome depends a lot on the judge who hears the case."

"If the birth mother loses custody, will Benny be put up for adoption?" Gib asked.

Maggie nodded. "Yes."

"Bee-bee," Alison said, extending her arms toward Benny. "Mine. Mine."

It was too much, it really was. Tears stung the back of Margaret's eyes and an achy sensation gripped her throat. The picture that Gib, Alison and Benjamin presented was so beautiful, so perfect, it was beyond description.

"Excuse me," Margaret said, getting to her feet. "I believe I'll use the powder room before we go to the petting zoo." She hurried across the room and disappeared down a hallway.

"You're a natural with those babies, Gib," Maggie said. "Do you have children of your own?"

"I have a grown daughter and two grandkids."

Maggie nodded. "Your experience shows. Not only that, but Alison and Benjamin sense that you're comfortable with them. They're both very contented."

"Alison is a heart stealer," Gib said, smiling. He shifted his gaze to Benjamin, who was still looking directly at him. Gib's smile faded. "And this little guy is no slouch in the heart-stealing department, either."

"I know." Maggie sighed. "There are so many people who won't even consider adopting him because he's a drug baby. They're afraid there will be far-reaching ramifications from his being addicted at birth."

"Benny deserves a loving home," Gib said quietly, "just as Alison did, as all children do."

Margaret remained in the doorway to the living room, having just heard the last words Gib had spoken. Her heart was racing and her emotions threatened to once again overwhelm her.

What a complex man, she thought. Gibson McKinley was a wealthy, savvy businessman who knew how to survive in the highly competitive world of newspaper publishing. He played the courting game required to woo and win advertisers, wore a tuxedo like a second skin and dined with the rich and famous.

But Gib was also a man who looked terrific in jeans and a sport shirt. A man who had suggested an outing to a dusty, noisy, smelly petting zoo. A man who appeared so *right* with Alison and Benjamin tucked safely in his arms.

Gib McKinley was the man who had made her feel so alive, so beautiful, when they'd made love together. A man who knew how to temper his physical strength with infinite gentleness, assuring her pleasure before seeking his own.

So many layers, so many facets, Margaret thought. As she discovered more and more about Gib, she embraced each new piece to the complicated puzzle that he was, putting it carefully in place to hopefully know the total man. A man who had become very, very important to her.

Oh, dear heaven, Margaret thought, taking a trembling breath, was she—please, no!—was she falling in love with him?

Chapter Eleven

The petting zoo was being held beneath a huge blue-and-white-striped tent enclosed by a three-foot-high white picket fence.

Gib paid the admission at the gate, then lifted Alison from Margaret's arms to his own as they entered the crowded enclosure.

"I don't know about this," Gib said, frowning. "I'm afraid that Alison will get knocked over."

Margaret swept her gaze around the tent. There were two lambs, three baby goats, a multitude of rabbits, several puppies and kittens, fluffy chicks and squealing piglets wandering across the sawdust-covered floor. Attendants wearing blue-and-white-striped aprons were keeping a close watch over the animals and exuberant children.

"Well, put Alison down," Margaret said. "She'll make up her own mind quickly enough."

Gib set Alison on her feet and she immediately stuck her thumb in her mouth as she stayed close to Gib's side.

"Let her look things over," Margaret said, raising her voice to be heard above the cacophony. "Goodness, it's hot in here."

Margaret slid a glance at Gib, who was watching Alison intently.

Had Gib been aware of how quiet she'd been during the drive from Maggie's house to the mall? she wondered. Was he even now speculating on what might have been occupying her thoughts?

She'd been attempting to deal with the emotions that had assaulted her as she'd watched Gib holding Alison and Benjamin, and she'd been shaken to the core by the depth of her feelings for Gib.

Instead of determining by day's end if she and Gibson could actually move backward to being just friends, she was now faced with the possibility that she'd moved forward instead. Was she falling in love with Gibson McKinley? Was he capturing her heart, inch by emotional inch? Oh, why didn't she know the answer?

"Kitty," Alison said around her thumb.

"Would you like to pet the kitty?" Margaret said. She reached down and took Alison's hand. "Shall we go closer, sweetheart?"

As Margaret and Alison took tentative steps toward the animals, Gib stayed where he was at the edge of the tent.

Was Margaret upset with him because he had hardly spoken to her after leaving Maggie's? he thought. He hadn't meant to ignore Margaret, but he'd been consumed by warring emotions.

Benjamin. He couldn't believe how difficult it had been to hand that baby boy back to Maggie, realizing he would probably never see the little guy again. It had felt so damn good, so right, sitting there with Alison and Benny in his arms. Then he'd looked up to see Margaret coming toward them, then settling next to them to complete the picture.

Oh, hell, this was crazy.

What was the matter with him?

"Oh, dear," Margaret said, snapping Gib back to attention.

Alison had wrapped both arms around a lamb's neck and was holding fast.

"Mine," Alison yelled. "Mine. Kitty. Kitty. Kitty."

A teenage attendant hurried over and bent to speak to Alison.

"Let go of the lamb, baby," she said. "Okay?"

"Mine!" Alison hollered.

The lamb began to back up, taking a determined Alison with it.

"Alison," Margaret said, "come on, sweetheart, you have to let go."

Gib chuckled and stepped closer, gripping Alison

around the waist. He lifted her into the air, and she shrieked in anger and kicked her feet.

"Gibson," Margaret said, laughing, "we're out of here right now."

"Well," the teenager said, smiling, "if you don't know what to get your daughter next Christmas, Mom and Dad, you can buy her a lamb that she'll think is a kitty."

Margaret smiled weakly at the girl, then hurried after Gib, who was trying to console a furious, wailing Alison. The toddler screamed all the way to the car, not coming up for a breath until she was in her car seat and Margaret offered her a Sippee cup of juice.

"No," Alison said, then grabbed the cup and poked it in her mouth.

Margaret and Gib got into the front seat, closed the doors of the vehicle and sighed.

"That was a disaster," Margaret said.

"No joke," Gib said, shaking his head.

They looked at each other and burst into laughter.

"That fiasco ranks right up there with the cherry tomato," Gib said, smiling. He paused, his grin fading. "The attendant thought we were Alison's parents...not grandparents...her mom and dad."

"Don't take it personally," Margaret said, surprised at the cross sound to her voice. "It was an honest mistake."

"Hey, I'm not complaining. I'm very flattered. Today of all days is a perfect time for someone to see me as a dad, not a granddad."

"What's so momentous about today?"

"It's my birthday. I'm officially fifty."

Margaret reached over to place one hand on Gib's arm.

"Why didn't you tell me? I would have baked a birthday cake and we could have celebrated your special day."

"I was attempting to pretend it wasn't here, just get through it, then wake up tomorrow with it behind me. Now? I don't know. Fifty doesn't seem all that bad, or even that old. I have you and Alison to thank for making me feel young. You two...and Benjamin."

Margaret dropped her hand and cocked her head slightly to one side.

"Benjamin?" she said.

Gib nodded, then met Margaret's questioning gaze.

"Yes," he said quietly. "Benny. The little scrapper really grabbed hold of my heart, Margaret. I won't be able to forget him very quickly, or easily, believe me."

He drew one thumb gently down Margaret's cheek.

"Margaret, I want you to know that because of what I felt when I held Benny, then scooped Alison up onto my lap, I...well, I understand much better—very clearly, in fact—why you adopted Alison."

Margaret's eyes filled with sudden, unexpected tears.

"Thank you, Gib," she whispered.

Her heart and mind were racing. What exactly was he saying to her? Was he envisioning himself as a *father*, rather than a grandfather?

"*I* couldn't do what you're doing," Gib went on, "but I just wanted you to know I truly understand why you made the choice you did."

A cold fist seemed to grip Margaret's heart and a knot tightened in her stomach.

Well, she thought, back to reality. Her *friend* Gibson now understood her life's choice. Her *friend* Gibson would be around until he got bored and restless with her restricted existence, then that would be that. So be it.

She felt as though she could cry for three hours straight.

Oh, what was the matter with her?

This better not be symptomatic of falling in love with Gib. It just better not.

Gib glanced at the rear seat where Alison was sipping happily on her cup, no worse for wear for having been denied ownership of a lamb.

"Look," he said, turning to Margaret again, "my house is only a mile or so from here. Why don't we go over there and have some ice cream?"

"All right," Margaret said, managing to produce a small smile. "You didn't have a cake, but the least we can do is have ice cream to celebrate your birthday."

"Absolutely." Gib laughed. "Especially since I've decided to finally acknowledge the fact that it *is* my birthday.'' He shook his head. ''I can't believe the way I was fighting becoming fifty. What a jerk.''

''But you've changed your views on the subject now,'' Margaret said as Gib started the car. ''That's what is important.''

''Yes, I suppose you're right,'' he said, driving out of the parking lot. ''I'll take comfort in knowing that I was a short-term jerk.''

Ten minutes later Gib parked in the driveway of a large, two-story house. He carried Alison into the house, while Margaret toted the diaper bag. In the living room Margaret stopped dead in her tracks.

''Don't put Alison down,'' she said.

''What?''

Margaret swept one hand through the air. ''It's a lovely room, Gib, but it won't be for long if you turn Alison loose. Let me put the knickknacks up and collect the magazines from the coffee table. All right?''

''Sure. You have a better eye for what is potential trouble. Help yourself.''

As Margaret hurried around the room, Gib talked to Alison to keep the toddler's attention. But while he went on and on about the wonderful petting zoo, he realized that his mind was splintered. Part of him was chattering at Alison. Another section of his brain was registering the fact that his house in its oh-so-perfect condition was not one bit welcoming to a little girl, or a family.

Was that why Betsy never stayed very long when she brought the kids over to visit? Was his daughter exhausted after a half hour of attempting to keep busy fingers from disturbing her father's "museum"?

This house, Gib thought, was not a home.

"There," Margaret said. "That should do it, if I keep a close eye on Alison. I need to change her diaper."

"There's a leather sofa in my office that Betsy always uses to change her kids. It's to the right there. I'll meet you in the kitchen. It's straight down the hall."

After Margaret changed Alison, they headed for the kitchen.

The more she saw of Gib's house, Margaret thought, the more aware she became that it shouted the fact that a man lived there. The furniture and accessories were all extremely masculine. Any woman Gib brought here would definitely get the message that she was simply visiting, and was not meant to become too comfortable in Gibson McKinley's domain.

By the time Margaret and Alison entered the kitchen, Gib had placed a booster seat on one of the chairs at the table, explaining he had it on hand for his grandson. His granddaughter was too young still for a high chair.

The trio settled at the table, Margaret spooning ice cream into Alison's mouth. The baby leaned forward to eagerly receive every bite.

"Margaret," Gib said suddenly, "why did you say you had no desire to remarry?"

Margaret looked over at him in surprise. "Where did that come from?"

"I don't know. I guess it has been in the back of my mind. You might have pursued a long-forgotten career dream after you became a widow, but you chose to donate your musical talent to underprivileged children. You're obviously happy in the role of mother. I assume the same holds true of being a wife. It doesn't make sense that you wouldn't be receptive to the idea of marriage."

Margaret shrugged. "It's nothing complicated, Gib. What Jack and I had wasn't perfect, because I don't believe there is any such thing as a perfect marriage. But what we shared all those years was special, rare, lovely. I can't imagine even coming close to that again. I prefer not to settle for less."

"But you *do* date."

"I did, past tense. The men I've been seeing have all called since I got Alison." Margaret laughed. "Each in their own way headed for the hills, never to be heard from again."

"You don't seem upset about it."

"Heavens, no. I fully expected them to do exactly that. My dates with them were pleasant social outings, nothing more. There are plenty of women out there in our age bracket who are not new mothers of a baby. Those men won't lack for companionship."

And not one of those men, she thought, would have told Alison she was a sweet and perfect Texas baby. Nor would they have had their heartstrings tugged by adorable little Benjamin. No, she had no desire to socialize with those men again. Not since Gib had entered her world.

"Why are *you* so against remarrying, Gib?" she said, then managed to take a bite of her own ice cream.

"Mum-mum," Alison said, smacking the table with her chubby hands.

"Yes, madam," Margaret said, smiling as she stuck the spoon in Alison's mouth.

Margaret looked at Gib again to see that he had pushed his bowl to one side and was frowning into space.

"Gib?"

He shifted his gaze to meet hers, but still didn't speak. Margaret raised her eyebrows questioningly.

"I've never told this to anyone," he said quietly. "I have a pat answer for reporters that I never intend to remarry, nor become involved in a serious relationship. Over the years it has been assumed and accepted that I never got over the loss of my wife, Elizabeth, in that car accident. The romantics of Houston society love that idea, I guess."

"But?"

"In strictest confidence?"

"Of course."

"Elizabeth was a secret drinker, Margaret. Life with her was a living hell. I did all I could to protect Betsy from Elizabeth's drunken rages, but…"

Gib sighed and shook his head.

"On the night she was killed, Elizabeth was on her way to meet one of her many lovers. She was drunk and missed a curve in the road. My connections kept the truth under wraps. I did it for Betsy's sake, not mine. By then I really didn't give a damn what people knew, but I wanted to shield my daughter from further pain.''

"Oh, Gib, I'm so very sorry. I...I thank you for trusting me, sharing this with me.''

"It was years ago. Marriage for me, however, does not bring back fond memories. As for trusting you? I do. Yes, I truly do.''

Their eyes met for a long moment, a special moment, a moment to be cherished and remembered. Their mutual trust was not to be taken lightly, and they both knew it. Hearts began to quicken as the embers of desire within them began to burn brighter, hotter.

"Damn," Alison said cheerfully.

Gib jerked as he was brought from the sensuous haze that had begun to consume his senses.

"Oh, cripe," he said. "I blew it. I said damn, didn't I?''

"Damn, damn, damn," Alison said, bobbing her head in rhythm to her nifty new word.

Margaret willed her heart to return to a normal tempo before she attempted to speak.

"Hopefully," she said, smiling, "she'll forget it if she doesn't hear it again. Otherwise, I won't be able to take her out of the house until she gets bored with how it sounds. You must admit, Gib, Alison does keep a person on their toes.''

"Alison," he said, no hint of a smile on his face, "is capable of bringing sunshine to the darkest day."

"What a lovely thing to say."

"It's true." Gib paused. "Do you suppose we could get a bow to stay in Alison's hair? That hair of hers seems determined to stick straight up. Maybe we should decorate it."

"Maybe," Margaret said.

She averted her eyes from Gib's, then busied herself feeding more ice cream to Alison.

We, Margaret's mind echoed. Why did Gib say things like that? He continually and maddeningly sent out conflicting messages, causing her to feel as though she was racing behind him, attempting to keep up with his signals that went one way, then another.

Gib had admitted that he'd been emotionally moved while holding Alison and Benjamin at Maggie's house.

In the next breath he'd quickly added that, oh, no, *he* wouldn't want any part of that type of existence, thank you very much.

Now he'd ricocheted back to contemplating in terms of *we,* as though he was an intricate and permanent part of the toddler's life.

The man was giving her the crazies. She was beginning to believe that she didn't understand Gibson McKinley at all.

And that was sad. Very, very sad.

Every time Gib shifted gears, a greater distance grew between them. A distance she was finding more and more difficult to close again. Gib was so confusing and utterly exhausting.

"All gone," Margaret said to Alison. "The ice cream is all gone, and now it's home and a nap for you, my sweet. Okay?"

"'Kay. 'Kay." Alison said, clapping her hands.

Margaret got to her feet and began to gather the bowls and spoons.

"Leave those, Margaret," Gib said. "I'll tend to them later. Do you really have to leave already? I have a box of toys I keep here for my grandchildren. Alison is welcome to play with whatever is in there."

"She's due for a nap," Margaret said. "She's smiling now, but a little gremlin will whisper in her ear, and she'll be cranky and ready to go to sleep in the next second. We need to head for home."

"All right," Gib said, rising.

The drive to Margaret's was silent, except for an occasional comment from Alison.

There was a strange tension in the air, an uneasy atmosphere that hung over Margaret and Gib like a dark, ominous cloud.

Was *she* responsible for this gloomy, edgy mood shift? Margaret wondered. Was her inner turmoil regarding her feelings for Gib spoiling the outing they'd had together?

Oh, she didn't know. In fact, she didn't know much of anything at the moment. What she wanted to do was to crawl into Alison's crib with the baby and take a nap!

When they reached Margaret's house, the trio had no sooner gone through the front door than Alison began to fuss and rub her eyes.

"Bingo," Margaret said. "The gremlin has whispered. Have a seat, Gib, while I put her down. Alison, say bye-bye."

"Mum-mum," Alison said, wrapping her arms around Margaret's neck.

Gib smiled. "Well, she has definitely got it straight about who her mum-mum is. She's still not steady on some of the other titles, though. Have a good nap, kiddo."

"Dough," Alison said sleepily. "Dough."

After settling the baby in the crib, Margaret pulled the door closed to within inches of the opening, then stood statue still in the hallway.

One more try, she decided, taking a deep breath. She hated the idea that she might have caused the awkward and distressing tension between her and Gib. She'd make one last attempt to salvage what had been a very nice day.

Margaret reentered the living room and went directly to the piano. A moment later a quiet rendition of "Happy Birthday" lilted through the air. Gib crossed the room to stand next to the piano.

"There," Margaret said, smiling when she'd finished the traditional song. "That should make you feel like the official birthday boy. I do wish you a very happy birthday, Gib."

With no readable expression on his face, Gib extended his hand to Margaret. She placed her hand in his and allowed him to draw her up and into his embrace.

He lowered his head and captured her mouth in a searing, nearly rough kiss that stole the very breath from her body.

She returned the kiss in total abandon, savoring the sensual sensations consuming her, carrying her away from the jumbled maze in her mind.

She didn't have to think, not now. All she needed to do was feel…and it was ecstasy. She didn't care that she and Gib were supposed to be only friends. It didn't matter that she was a confused, befuddled mess regarding Gibson McKinley.

All that was important at this moment was their kiss, this heated, exquisite, passion-evoking kiss.

Margaret, Gib's mind hummed. So many times during the hours they'd just spent together he'd wanted to touch her, caress the soft skin of her cheeks, sift the silken strands of her hair through his fingers.

And, oh, Lord, how he'd wanted to take her into his arms and kiss her.

He was on fire, the heat rocketing through his aroused body causing a coiled pain deep and low within him. Never before, *never*, had he desired a woman the way he did Margaret Madison.

Gib slid his hands down over Margaret's jeans-covered bottom, nestling her to the cradle of his hips. He shifted his hands upward to inch beneath the waistband of the knit top she wore, his fingers tingling as they met her dewy skin.

He wanted to make love with Margaret, the need so strong it was overpowering. The memories of their lovemaking beat against his brain, heightening his passion even more.

And the emotions, McKinley? a little voice in his mind nagged. What of them? What about the depth of his feelings for Margaret, the ever-growing caring, respect and...and love?

No!

He was *not* falling in love with Margaret Madison.

Gib broke the kiss, drew a ragged, raspy breath, then moved Margaret away from his heated, aching body. She slowly lifted her lashes, and he nearly groaned aloud as he saw the smoky hue of desire in her big brown eyes.

"I'm sorry," he said, his voice gritty. "That shouldn't have happened."

Margaret averted her eyes from Gib's, then fiddled with straightening her top smoothly over her jeans.

"No, it shouldn't have," she said, then lifted her head slowly to meet his gaze again. "We've...we've agreed to be just friends."

"Your lover, your partner, is supposed to be your best friend." Gib shook his head in self-disgust. "Forget it. I don't know why I said that."

"Well, it's true, but it doesn't apply in our case. We're not establishing our friendship as a foundation for anything more."

"Yes, I know. I know that. I apologize for kissing you, Margaret."

"I kissed you back, so I guess I owe you that same apology."

"Whatever," he said gruffly. "I'd better leave." Gib paused. "Listen, I realize how close you and Amy are, but I hope you understand that she's not to be told what I shared with you about my marriage, about Elizabeth. Amy would probably feel she shouldn't keep secrets from Blue and... Well, just don't tell anyone."

The sensuous haze still floating around Margaret disappeared as it was shoved aside by the rush of anger taking its place.

"Dear heaven, Gibson," she said, planting her hands on her hips. "Do you want me to sign a document in blood that says I won't divulge what you told me?"

"There's no reason to get angry," he said, frowning.

"No reason? You said you trusted me. I didn't take that lightly, not at all. Trust, truth, honesty are part of my inner values, of who I am."

Margaret wrapped her hands around her elbows in a protective gesture.

"But you don't really trust me at all, do you?" she said. "If you did, you wouldn't have just delivered your insulting little sermon about not talking about the secrets of your past. I'm not just angry, Gib, I'm also hurt that you felt it necessary to make certain I understand exactly what trust is."

"Margaret, I..." Gib said, extending one hand toward her.

Margaret stepped backward, out of his reach.

"Do you want to know what *I* think, Gibson?" she said. "I think that you don't trust *yourself.* Yes, that's it." She nodded. "It all makes sense now."

"What are you talking about?" he said, his voice rising.

"When you came into my life, Gib, you made certain that you had left the door open behind you so you could escape whenever you felt the need. You made it clear that you would be around only as long as it suited you."

"So?" he said, narrowing his eyes.

"You've admitted that Alison has taken hold of your heart. You even said that little Benjamin had pulled at your heartstrings. But in the next breath you were scrambling to say that a life with babies wasn't for you. Oh, no, no way would you do that routine again."

"Damn it, what's that got to do with your accusation that I don't trust myself?"

"I believe, Gibson McKinley, that you've never forgiven yourself for trusting in Elizabeth, for loving her, and then being so devastated by the nightmare of your marriage to her."

"You're crazy," he snapped.

"Am I? You're afraid to trust your feelings for me, Gib. For Alison. Even for little Benny. You move close, then closer, then you back off, saying marriage and babies are not your cup of tea.

"You can't get hurt that way, can you, Gib? If you don't listen to your inner voice, trust in the emotions that are yours, then you can't make another mistake like you did with Elizabeth.''

"That's enough,'' Gib said, a pulse beating in his temple. ''You're so off base, it's a crime.''

"No, I don't think I am,'' Margaret said quietly, sounding suddenly weary, drained. ''I feel sorry for you, Gib. You're not willing to take any risks or put your heart on the line for anyone, because of what happened to you years ago. Things within your grasp will just pass you by, because you don't have the courage to believe and trust in yourself.''

"I'm not listening to any more of this nonsense,'' he said, starting toward the door. ''I won't be back, Margaret.''

"I know that,'' she said softly. ''But, Gib?''

He yanked open the door, then half turned to scowl at her.

"What?'' he said.

"Did it ever occur to you that you might wake up one morning and realize you're totally alone? That you're very, very lonely?''

"The hell I will,'' he said, then left the house, slamming the door behind him.

Margaret stood in the suddenly silent room, her eyes filling with tears.

"Goodbye, Gibson,'' she whispered as two tears slid down her pale cheeks.

Chapter Twelve

Life was more confusing at fifty than it had been during his turbulent adolescence, Gib decided on Friday of the following week.

He leaned back in the chair in his office and felt a wave of exhaustion sweep over him.

He'd hardly slept since that last scene at Margaret's, spending the long, dark hours of the nights tossing and turning.

And *thinking*. Damn, he was sick to death of thinking, analyzing, dissecting everything Margaret had said to him. No, correct that. Everything Margaret Madison had *accused* him of.

At first he'd firmly denied there was any validity to Margaret's declarations. But as her words continued to echo over and over, he'd begun to question whether or not what Margaret had said was true.

Was he afraid of running the risks involved in a committed relationship because of what had happened in his marriage? *Was* he unable to trust and believe in himself because he'd made a terrible mistake in choosing Elizabeth as his life's partner?

Elizabeth had been an average social drinker, as he was, when he'd met her. After they were married and she became pregnant with Betsy, she'd stopped drinking completely, hadn't touched a drop in fear of harming the baby she was carrying.

But then it had all fallen apart.

Elizabeth's fantasy of motherhood was like playing dolls with a smiling, happy infant, and it burst like a balloon when colicky Betsy arrived. Elizabeth couldn't cope with the ongoing demands of her infant daughter, and began to attempt to drown her insecurities in liquor.

It had been Gib who had walked the floor with Betsy at night, then turned the baby over to a caregiver during the day. Elizabeth was off to play tennis, bridge, go shopping, or have long lunches with friends.

At social gatherings Elizabeth was beautiful, gracious, charming, and never left Gib's side. They were considered the perfect couple, and people sighed wistfully with envy at the match made in heaven.

They even had an incredibly wonderful daughter, who was obviously adored beyond measure by her parents. Elizabeth was heard exclaiming constantly to any audience who would listen about the intelligence and beauty of the McKinley offspring.

But at home, behind closed doors where no one could see, Elizabeth drank. She paid little attention to her daughter and more often than not raged in anger at Gib about everything.

Elizabeth was ill, Gib would tell himself. He had taken solemn wedding vows to stand by her in sickness and in health, for better, for worse. He begged her to seek help with her drinking problem. Elizabeth adamantly refused.

To divorce her, to take their child and leave, would be to admit he was unable to reach Elizabeth with his love.

To walk away from Elizabeth McKinley was to announce to the world that Gibson McKinley had failed.

Never again, Gib had promised himself. When Elizabeth had died in the fiery car crash, it had closed the door on years of living hell, a nightmare he would never risk repeating again.

Risk? Gib thought, lunging to his feet. *Had* his marriage caused him to lose faith in his own judgment? *Had* it resulted in his no longer trusting himself to believe in his feelings, his emotions, the whisperings from his heart, mind and soul?

Had Margaret Madison's words, which had cut him to the quick, been carrying the message of truth, adding salt to bleeding, emotional wounds?

Ah, hell, he didn't know. He was a mental mess, a confused, exhausted man of fifty.

Fifty, Gib thought, hooking one hand on the back of his neck. He'd finally gotten comfortable with this age, with the arrival of the dreaded birthday. He'd felt young and carefree, glad to be alive.

And the attendant at the petting zoo had thought he was Alison's daddy.

"Enough of this," Gib muttered. "I'm driving myself nuts."

He left his office, welcoming the loud noise that assaulted him the moment he opened the door. As he glanced around the newsroom, he spotted Amy at one of the desks. Gib ambled in her direction.

"Hello, Amy," he said when he finally stopped next to where she was busily typing on the computer.

"Hi, Gib." Amy glanced up at him, then did a double take. "Heavens, you look exhausted, as though *you're* the person who has a new little one in the house, instead of my mother."

"You could have gone all day long without saying *that*, Amy."

"Sorry." Amy paused. "But seriously, Gib, are you all right? You really look wiped out."

Gib shrugged. "I've had a bit of insomnia lately. It's nothing serious. It happens to everyone from time to time."

"Mmm," Amy said, continuing to stare at him.

"Cripe, Amy, quit looking at me like you're trying to decide whether or not to close the coffin."

"Now that," she said, laughing, "was funny."

"You sound a lot like your mother when you laugh," Gib said, no hint of a smile on his face. "I never noticed that before." He cleared his throat. "So! How *is* your mother? And Alison?"

Amy frowned. "You don't know? I thought my boss was dating my mom."

Gib slammed his hands flat on the desk and leaned toward Amy. She jumped in surprise at his sudden motion.

"I don't know what?" he said, a deep frown knitting his brows. "What don't I know about Margaret and Alison? Is something wrong with one of them? Both of them? For God's sake, Amy, talk to me."

Amy's eyes had widened in shock during Gib's tirade and her mouth had dropped open. She shook her head slightly and blinked.

"Goodness gracious, what is your problem? I wasn't insinuating that anything was wrong with my mom or Alison. I was merely wondering why you weren't in contact with them. The last I heard, you three were going to a petting zoo. I've been super busy and haven't connected with my mom so far this week."

Gib straightened and cleared his throat. "Oh."

"What's going on here?" Amy narrowed her eyes in concentration. "You can't sleep. Your nerves are obviously shot. You came unglued at the mere mention of my mother and baby sister. I do believe, Mr. McKinley, that *you* should be talking to *me*."

"In my office," Gib said, then spun around and strode away.

"What a bossy boss," Amy muttered, pressing keys on the computer to save her work. "However, I'll forgive him this time, because I most definitely want to hear what's on his mind."

When Amy entered Gib's office, she closed the door, then sat in the chair opposite his desk. Gib was sitting behind the desk, glaring at the eraser on the end of a pencil.

"Hello? Hello?" Amy said brightly. "I'm here." She folded her hands in her lap. "And I'm all ears, Mr. McKinley, sir."

"Mmm." Gib tossed the pencil onto the desk and looked at Amy. "Amy, have you ever wondered why I've never remarried?"

"Is *that* what we're talking about?"

"Just answer the question."

"Good grief," Amy said, "you're so grumpy, Gib."

"Amy..." Gib said, a warning tone to his voice.

"All right, all right, let me think. I suppose it crossed my mind at some point. There are people who believe that you're still mourning your wife, but I don't buy that theory."

"You don't? Why not?"

"Because it doesn't fit who I know you to be. You're too strong, dynamic, too much of a go-getter to be hung up in the past. You would have grieved for your wife, then moved forward."

"Well, your mother believes just the opposite," Gib said quietly. "She's convinced that my behavior today is influenced tremendously by my past."

"My mom thinks that you're still in love with your wife?"

"No, not that I'm in love with Elizabeth, or her

memory, but that the years spent in that marriage are controlling my actions in the present.''

''You've lost me, Gib. If you're not still in love with Elizabeth, then what's the problem here?'' Amy paused. ''You found marriage too restricting? You like being a playboy?''

''I am *not* a playboy!''

''Don't yell at me! You're the one who wanted to have this discussion, and for the life of me I can't figure out what we're discussing.''

''Your mother and I had a falling out, all right? A doozy of an argument, okay? She accused me of allowing my past to dictate my present and future.''

''Is that true?''

''No. Yes. No.'' Gib flung out his arms. ''Hell, I don't know. Thanks to your mother I'm lucky to know what my name is, or what day of the week this is. That woman has scrambled my brain.''

''Oh...my...gosh,'' Amy said, her eyes as big as saucers. ''You're in love with my mother.''

''I am not,'' Gib yelled.

''Okay,'' Amy said, smiling sweetly, ''you're not.''

''Of course I'm not.'' Gib paused. ''Am I?''

Amy shrugged. ''Beats me. All I know is, all the symptoms are there. The scrambled brain is the topper. Yes, sir, when you get all the way to your brain being scrambled, it's usually a done deal. You're in love.''

''Oh, Lord,'' Gib said, dragging both hands down his face. ''I need a vacation. A shrink. A brain transplant." He glowered at Amy. "If I was in love, Mrs. Bishop, I sure as hell would be aware of that fact."

Amy pointed one finger in the air. "I beg to differ with that statement. You would not necessarily realize that you were in love, because love is a sneaky little bugger. Hence the scrambled brain. What I would recommend is that you take some time—private, quiet time—to sort through the scramble."

Gib nodded, still frowning.

"This is a pretty complicated situation, Gib," Amy went on, "because my mother is a package deal. She comes with a toddler. Most women her age don't have a baby in tow."

"No joke."

"You're kind of old to start the diaper brigade all over again, you know what I mean?" Amy examined her fingernails. "Yep, there are diapers, gunky food, temper tantrums, sticky fingers…the list is just endless."

"And there is a child's laughter," Gib said quietly, "that is more beautiful than tinkling bells, and little hands that wrap around your neck so trustingly. There are big blue eyes and funny blond hair that sticks up in all directions, and a mother who gazes at that baby with so much love shining in her eyes that it makes a person feel humble to be witnessing it."

Amy got to her feet.

"I think," she said gently, "that you're beginning to unscramble the scramble, Gib. Good luck."

She left the office, closing the door behind her with a muted click.

That evening after darkness had fallen with a gentle hush and the stars had begun to sparkle in the Texas sky, Gib went for a walk.

He strolled, shoving his hands into his pockets as he ambled along the sidewalks in his neighborhood. For the first twenty minutes he allowed his imagination to float free as he glanced at the houses with lights glowing behind drawn drapes.

In his imaginings he produced a happy family for each structure, each *home*. His mind's eye saw some people eating dinner, others watching television, a father helping a son with his homework, a mother reading a story to a giggling little girl.

Then slowly, reluctantly, he brought his thoughts back to center on himself.

And Margaret.

Gib sighed, feeling suddenly tired, as though the weight of the world was resting on his shoulders.

Did it ever occur to you that you might wake up one morning and realize you're totally alone? That you're very, very lonely?

Margaret's words slammed against Gib's brain, causing him to stumble slightly from their impact.

He walked on, reliving that last angry scene with Margaret, hearing her accusations and his furious denial of her charges.

He walked on, squaring off against the demons of

his past, slaying the dragons of misery, disillusion-ment and failure.

He walked on, his step quickening, his exhaustion evaporating as he shed the heavy, emotional load that was crushing him.

He walked on, and he knew, with a sense of peace and rightness, that he was deeply and irrevocably in love with Margaret Madison.

Gib looked up to find that he was once again in front of his own house. He stared at the impressive, expensive structure and acknowledged the fact that it had been a house—not a home—for more years than he cared to remember.

Margaret had a home. It was filled with love and laughter and sunshine.

And Margaret had a life that was overflowing with the same treasures, because she had been willing to reach out and embrace the present and future and all they would bring to her. She'd laid her heart and soul on the line, and had been rewarded with the im-measurable joy of a sweet and perfect Texas baby...Alison.

But he had turned his back on Margaret and Alison and walked away.

And he was very, very lonely.

Gib entered the house and slouched into his fa-vorite chair in the living room. Glancing around the showcase-perfect room, he frowned.

He was in love, he thought glumly. He was honest-to-goodness in love with a beautiful, intelligent, un-believably fantastic woman.

He should be on cloud nine, singing from the roof-tops, shouting the message in the form of headlines in his own newspaper.

Gib drew a ragged breath.

He wanted to marry Margaret, stay by her side until death parted them. He wanted to be Alison's father, protecting and guiding her as she grew to womanhood. He loved that Texas baby, just as he loved his Betsy. He wanted to live with his family in a house that was truly a home.

Gib laughed, a rough, sharp-edged sound that echoed tauntingly in the silent room.

"Is there anything else you want, McKinley?" he said aloud.

Dear God, how was he going to convince Margaret that he truly loved her and Alison?

How was he going to get Margaret to reverse her stand on not wishing to marry again?

How was he going to make Margaret believe that, yes, he was, at fifty years old, embracing, savoring, treasuring, as the precious gift it was, the role of *father*, not just a grandfather who lived across town?

Gib suddenly realized that he hadn't eaten any dinner. He got to his feet and started toward the kitchen, his brows knitted in concentration.

As much as he would like to get in his car and drive to Margaret's right now, he wasn't going to do it. This was not the time to act on emotional impulse, which would probably result in him saying and doing something totally lame.

He had to take this slow and easy, think it through,

pick his words carefully before presenting them to
Margaret. His entire future happiness was at stake.
He mustn't do anything rash.

Patience and planning, he thought with a decisive
nod. That was what was called for here. When he
was steadier on his emotional feet, he'd go to Margaret Madison and ask her if she'd do him the honor
of becoming his wife.

Late that night Margaret threw back the blankets
and left her bed, furious over the fact that she was
once again unable to sleep.

She checked on a peaceful Alison, then went into
the kitchen to prepare yet another middle-of-the-
night serving of warm milk.

With the mug in hand she walked slowly into the
living room, making her way forward by the dim
glow from the kitchen light.

Gibson McKinley was driving her right over the
edge of sanity, she fumed. She was thoroughly exhausted, due to lack of sleep caused by the haunting
memories of Gib.

She did fairly well during the day while busy with
Alison, but at night, alone in her bed, Gib came to
call in vivid images in her mind's eye.

She missed him, she knew it, and was none too
pleased with herself over that fact. She hadn't realized how many wonderful memories they'd made together until the remembrances began marching
through her mind like pesky soldiers.

"Go away, Gibson," she said aloud. "Go away and leave me alone."

As she was about to settle on the sofa to drink her milk, she stubbed her bare toe on something she couldn't see.

"Oh," she gasped as pain shot through her toe and up her foot. "Ow. Oh, damn it."

Setting the mug on the coffee table, she sank onto the sofa, then bent over to rub her throbbing toe. Her hand came to rest on something hard that was protruding from beneath the sofa. Pulling it free, she leaned back against the cushions, holding the culprit in both hands.

It was the toy typewriter Gibson had given to Alison.

"Oh, dear heaven," Margaret whispered, staring at the toy.

It was too much, it really was. It was the crowning blow, the final straw.

Margaret clutched the typewriter to her breasts and burst into tears.

She couldn't fight it anymore, or rationalize it away. It was too big, powerful and overwhelming. There was nowhere to run to, to hide from the truth.

She was in love with Gibson McKinley.

"Oh-h-h," Margaret wailed. "I really hate myself for loving that man."

She sniffled as she rested her chin on the brightly colored plastic toy.

When had she lost control of her emotions? she wondered frantically. How had this happened? Oh, what difference did it make? There was no denying the fact that she had fallen in love with a man who was not in love with her.

Even worse was the realization that if Gib *did* have feelings for her, it wouldn't change the outcome. Gibson was not about to nurture emotions for a woman who had a toddler to raise.

No way. Nohow.

Gib was mired in the nightmares of his past, in the disaster that had been his marriage to Elizabeth. He would walk away from any attachment he might have for her and Alison.

It was hopeless.

She had to forget about Gib somehow, erase from her mind the image of his ruggedly handsome face, the sound of his voice, the rumble of his laughter, the aroma that was uniquely his.

She mustn't dwell on the sweet remembrances of their lovemaking, or envision how right he looked every time he held Alison, or the beautiful picture he'd presented with Alison and Benjamin wrapped protectively in his strong arms.

Benjamin. That baby had touched Gib's heart, yet Gib had had the willpower to walk away from the infant. Alison had claimed a portion of Gib's heart, as well, but Gib had turned his back on Alison, too.

And Gibson McKinley cared for her, she knew he did, she just knew it.

But Gib was tough, and Gib was in control, and Gib was gone forever, without looking over his shoulder for one last glimpse of her.

"Well, fine," Margaret said, smacking the typewriter onto the cushion next to her. "If he can do it, so can I."

She got to her feet and fresh tears filled her eyes. "But, oh, God, how long is it going to take?"

Chapter Thirteen

The next afternoon Margaret took Alison shopping for a pair of new shoes. The baby cooperated beautifully, but was obviously more entranced by the tissue paper and box once the purchase was made.

Back in the car, Margaret realized they were at a mall only blocks from Maggie's house.

"Mmm," Margaret said thoughtfully, turning the key in the ignition.

She had been planning on calling Maggie that evening. Maggie had a wonderful grandmother-type woman, Justine, who baby-sat whenever Maggie needed to leave the house. Justine knew Alison, and Alison knew and liked her. And since Margaret was contemplating resuming her free piano lessons at the community center one afternoon a week to start, Justine would be the perfect choice of a sitter. Her intention had been to telephone Maggie and ask for Justine's phone number.

Miss Manners wouldn't approve, Margaret supposed, but it would be so easy to pop into Maggie's, even though she hadn't called the foster mother first. Maggie was so easygoing that surely she wouldn't mind.

The decision made, Margaret drove to Maggie's neighborhood and parked in the woman's driveway. A few minutes later she was on the front porch with Alison propped on her hip, still clutching the coveted shoe box. Margaret pressed the doorbell.

Maggie opened the door and smiled.

"Well, hello," she said. "Isn't this a pleasant surprise?"

"I should have called first. Is this a convenient time for us to drop in?"

"Absolutely," Maggie said, smiling. "This is our day for company, and I'm delighted. There's someone here that you know."

"Oh?"

Margaret glanced over her shoulder to see if there was a vehicle parked at the curb that she hadn't noticed. Her breath caught and her heart quickened.

Gib? she thought. Was that Gibson's car? No, it couldn't be. What earthly reason would Gibson McKinley have for being at Maggie's house?

"Margaret?" Maggie said. "Are you going to come in off the porch?"

Margaret snapped her head back around. "What? Oh, yes, of course."

"Shoes," Alison said, sticking one foot straight out. "Pretty."

"Yes, I see your pretty new shoes, Alison," Maggie said.

Margaret stepped into the house, hardly breathing as she kept her gaze riveted on Alison's airborne foot.

"Hello, Margaret."

Oh, good Lord, Margaret thought, that was Gib's voice, that marvelous, deep, rumbly voice that was so achingly familiar.

Margaret turned slowly toward the sound, her eyes widening at what she saw.

Gib was standing across the room with Benjamin tucked in the crook of his arm. The baby was dressed in a miniature baseball suit and his dark eyes were looking up at Gib.

Yes, there stood Gibson McKinley, the man she was so very much in love with. She couldn't handle this. She wasn't emotionally prepared to see him. She wanted to dash out the door, run away as fast as she could...away from Gib.

"Hello, Gib," she managed to say, her voice not quite steady. "I had no idea you were here." She paused and frowned. "*Why* are you here?" She paused again. "I'm sorry. That was rude. It's none of my business. I... How are you?"

In love with you, Gib thought, unable to tear his gaze from Margaret. *Oh, yes, hello, my beautiful*

Margaret and my precious Texas baby. There they were…his future, his family. *If* he could convince Margaret to marry him. *If* Margaret Madison loved him as he loved her.

"I'm fine," Gib said. "And you? And Alison?"

"Fine. Yes, we're fine."

Maggie looked at Margaret, Gib, back to Margaret, then cleared her throat to hide a knowing smile.

"Do sit down, Margaret," Maggie said with the sweep of an arm. "Alison, let me have a better look at your pretty new shoes. And, oh, my, don't you have a very special box there?"

Margaret set Alison on her feet, then sank onto the sofa. Her heart was racing with such a wild tempo, she could hear the echo of it hammering in her ears.

This was insane, she thought. A nightmare. She'd dropped by a foster mother's house to obtain the telephone number of a baby-sitter and bumped smack-dab into Gibson McKinley? It was crazy. So was the fact that Gib was standing there holding Benjamin just as naturally as you please. What was going on here?

"Benjamin looks well," Margaret said, smiling slightly. "That's an adorable outfit he's wearing."

"Gib bought him that baseball suit," Maggie said, sitting down in a chair and lifting Alison onto her lap. "I put it right on Benjamin. It's so cute."

"I saw it in a store," Gib said. "I purchased one just like it when my grandson was born. I recognized it and thought of Benny." He shrugged. "So here I am."

"Right," Margaret said, nodding slowly. "Babies being at the front of your mind the majority of the time, of course."

"Do I hear a touch of sarcasm there, Margaret?" Gib said, raising his eyebrows.

"Would you two like to be alone?" Maggie said pleasantly. "I'd be happy to leave the room."

"No," Margaret said. "I'm sorry, Maggie. We're guests in your home and... I just came by to ask for Justine's phone number. I'm thinking of giving piano lessons again. It would only be one afternoon a week, and Justine would be the perfect baby-sitter for Alison."

"That's a marvelous idea." Maggie got to her feet, holding Alison. "I'll go get the number for you."

"Oh, but..." Margaret started, then stopped speaking.

"Oh, but what?" Gib said as Maggie disappeared from view. "You don't want to be alone with me?"

Margaret met Gib's gaze directly, lifting her chin.

"No, actually, Gib, I don't," she said. "We have nothing to say to each other, and I don't feel up to engaging in idle chitchat with you."

"I see. Well, we could talk about babies. That's a safe enough topic. Benjamin has gained four ounces since we saw him last, and he's sleeping a little better. I heard Alison say 'shoes.' That's a new word for her."

Margaret got to her feet.

"I don't understand this," she said, wrapping her

hands around her elbows. "I don't understand *you*. The truth, Gib. Why are you here?"

"Because I care about Benjamin," he said. "I care about how he's doing, what's going to happen to him in the future. I no longer intend to ignore the feelings I have for this baby. He's important to me."

"He is?" Margaret blinked. "Really?"

"Really. My coming here, seeing and holding Benny, buying him a baseball suit, is risky business, wouldn't you say? This little guy is a heart stealer, and the day will come when he's adopted and I'll have no way to see him again. But I'm running that *risk*, Margaret, because he's worth it. I'm probably going to have my heart smashed to smithereens when Benny leaves Maggie's, but so be it."

"None of what you're saying sounds like you, Gib," Margaret said. "This is all very confusing."

"I listened to what you said to me, what you accused me of."

Alison came back into the room and headed straight for Gib.

"Think about it," Gib said to Margaret, then directed his attention to Alison. "Hi, kiddo. How's my Texas baby?"

"Dough. Dough," Alison said, dropping the shoe box and raising her arms. "Up."

Gib hunkered down, scooped Alison into his free arm and straightened again.

"Kitty," Alison said, patting Gib on the cheek. "Doggy. Da-da."

Gib laughed. "That about covers it."

"Here we go," Maggie said, returning to the room. She handed Margaret a piece of paper. "Justine's telephone number."

"Thank you," Margaret said, tucking the paper into her purse.

"My goodness, Gib," Maggie said, smiling, "don't you have a lovely armload there."

"It's just about perfect," Gib said, looking at Margaret.

"We must be going," Margaret said, averting her eyes from Gib's intense stare. "Say bye-bye, Alison."

Alison threw her arms around Gib's neck.

"Mine," the baby said. "Mine, mine, mine."

Oh, Alison, please, Margaret silently begged. *Don't do this to your falling-apart-at-the-seams mommy. I have to get out of this room.*

Maggie received Margaret's pleading look and untangled Alison from Gib's neck by offering her the forgotten shoe box. Margaret retrieved Alison from Maggie's arms, mumbled her goodbyes and beat a hasty retreat.

"Well, Benjamin," Gib said, looking at the infant, who was still snuggled contently in the crook of his arm, "it would appear that I've got my work cut out for me. Big time."

"If you're attempting to accomplish what I think you are in regard to Margaret," Maggie said, "I'd say you're absolutely right."

Benjamin hiccuped, as though adding his affirmative vote.

"Thanks, little buddy," Gib said, chuckling. "You're not very encouraging, you know."

"You're so good with Benjamin," Maggie said, sitting back down. "He responds to your voice and he's very calm and relaxed when you hold him. You have a positive effect on him, Gib."

"That doesn't even begin to describe what he does for me. I think he looks like me, don't you?"

Maggie nodded. "He could very easily be mistaken for your son."

"My son," Gib said, gazing at the baby. "You know, Maggie, I'm beginning to believe that that just might not be a mistake at all."

"What are you saying?"

"I'm not sure at the moment. There are a great many changes taking place in my life right now. I've got a lot to think about."

"I hope you find the answers you're seeking, Gib, and that you'll be happy."

"I thought I *was* happy, until Margaret Madison came into my life. She has shown me a whole new world that I'd forgotten was there. Benjamin, listen up. Women are very wise creatures. Very wise and very wonderful."

Maggie laughed. "Memorize that, Benny."

"Yes, Benjamin," Gib said. "Don't wait until you're fifty years old to figure it out like I did."

With a sigh of relief Margaret sank onto the sofa in her living room. Alison was down for a nap and the house was blessedly silent.

Leaning her head back on the top of the sofa, Margaret closed her eyes as she mentally replayed the scene at Maggie's.

My goodness, Gib, don't you have a lovely armload there.

It's just about perfect.

Margaret opened her eyes, lifted her head and pressed her hands to her flushed cheeks.

Just *about* perfect?

Gib had looked at her when he'd said that, his eyes seeming to pin her in place, making it nearly impossible to breathe.

What had Gib been trying to say to her? she wondered frantically. That it would take *her* being next to him to make it totally perfect? Or was she reading too much into a simple statement that had been casually spoken?

And then there was Gib's rambling discourse about running the *risk* of becoming attached to Benjamin, and that he had listened to what she'd said.

A painful headache began to throb in her temples and she massaged them, closing her eyes again.

She'd been stunned and flustered to find Gib at Maggie's. It had been a sincere desire on Gib's part to see Benjamin, and was not some sort of performance for her benefit, because he'd had no idea that she was going to be there.

Oh, it was all so confusing. Gib's actions, along with what he'd said, were adding to the jumbled maze in her mind. She already had enough to deal with regarding Gibson McKinley.

Realizing that she was in love with Gib was devastating, causing her tremendous emotional distress. Gib was adding to her turmoil by saying and doing things that were impossible to decipher in her present state of mind.

A wave of nausea swept over Margaret and the pain in her head increased.

"Oh-h-h," she said. "I feel rotten."

She stretched out on the sofa, hoping she'd be as good as new when Alison woke from her nap.

"I'll be fine," she mumbled.

But she wasn't.

Alison slept longer than usual and woke crying, instead of chattering happily in her crib.

With her head still aching and her stomach churning, Margaret hurried to Alison's room to discover that the baby had vomited.

Before she could tend to a weeping Alison, Margaret had to dash to the bathroom to be sick, which increased her headache even more.

The following hours were a blur of misery to Margaret. Alison was unable to keep down more than a few swallows of juice and Margaret was in the same condition.

Alison clung to Margaret, alternating between crying and dozing, the baby's cheeks flushed with fever. Margaret walked the floor with the heavy bundle, every step causing pain to shoot through her head and her stomach to roll.

Thoroughly exhausted, Margaret finally climbed onto her bed with Alison across her chest. Tears filled Margaret's eyes as Alison held on tightly, sobbing as though her little heart would break.

"Oh, baby," Margaret whispered, two tears sliding down the sides of her face to the pillow. "I'm sorry, so sorry. I'm not doing a good job of taking care of you right now at all. I'm doing the best I can but, dear God, it's not enough."

"Mum-mum," Alison said with a hiccuping sob. "Ma-ma."

"I'm here, I'm here," Margaret said, wrapping her arms more tightly around her daughter. "Oh, no," she said as a bout of nausea struck her.

Margaret slid from beneath Alison and ran for the bathroom. Alison cried at full volume. When Margaret emerged from the bathroom, a wave of dizziness swept over her and she dropped to her knees.

"Mum-mum," Alison screamed, reaching out her arms. "Mum-mum. Ma-ma."

Margaret crawled on her hands and knees to the bed, then pulled herself up to stretch out again, holding fast to Alison.

She had to get some help. She was so ill she was endangering Alison's safety. How could she tend to her precious daughter when she could hardly stand up herself?

She looked at the clock, amazed to see that it was after ten, having no idea where the hours of the evening had gone.

Think, she ordered herself. Amy. Amy would come. No, no, Amy and Blue were in Dallas at a horse sale.

Maggie. No, Maggie had Benjamin, and couldn't leave him.

Think.

She had lots of friends. They'd all been eager to attend the baby shower, and share in the joy of Margaret becoming Alison's mother.

A friend, she thought suddenly, is someone you could telephone at two in the morning, say "I need you," and they'd come, without asking why.

A multitude of faces flashed before her eyes like pictures in a movie, faces of her friends, but...

A sob caught in Margaret's throat and black dots danced before her eyes.

She couldn't call any of them, she thought with a chill of panic. It was one thing to go out to lunch, or shopping, or attend a baby shower, and quite another to step in and take charge of a sick mother and child.

She'd told Gib her definition of a friend, she thought foggily, on that night they'd been together just before she'd brought Alison home.

What had he said in reply?

Oh, she couldn't remember.

Margaret, please, think.

Yes, yes, it was coming back to her now. Gib had said, *I'd like to believe that we're friends. I would* come at two in the morning if you needed me, and I wouldn't ask why.

"Ma-ma," Alison whimpered.

"I don't know if he still means it, Alison," she said, "after all that has happened, but..."

Nestling Alison even closer to her, Margaret reached for the telephone receiver with a trembling hand. Hardly able to see past the tears filling her eyes, she pressed the numbers. Alison cried louder, clutching handfuls of Margaret's blouse.

The telephone began to ring on the other end of the line.

Please, Gib, Margaret silently begged. Oh, please.

"Hello?"

"Gib? It's Margaret," she said, a sob catching in her throat. "I need you."

"I'm on my way."

The dial tone hummed and Margaret dropped the receiver onto the bed.

She wrapped her arms around a wailing Alison and cried along with her.

"He's coming," Margaret said, sobbing. "Gib's coming to us, baby, because we need him, and he didn't even ask why."

Chapter Fourteen

Gib drove above the speed limit, his heart thundering and his grip on the steering wheel tightening to the extent that his knuckles were white.

Margaret, he mentally telegraphed, *hang on, my darling. I'm coming as quickly as I can.*

Dear God, the sound of her voice on the telephone had sent chills of fear spiraling through him. Margaret had been crying and he'd heard Alison wailing so pitifully in the background.

Margaret was ill, or hurt. Or Alison was ill, or hurt. Or... *Hurry, drive faster, McKinley.* The woman he was in love with and the child he loved as though she was his own needed him *now.*

After what seemed like an eternity, with every vehicle he got caught behind on the road going in slow motion, Gib swung his car into Margaret's driveway.

Moments later he was running across the lawn and up onto the porch. He tried the door and found it locked, pressed the doorbell with more force than was necessary, then pushed it again, then again.

"Come on, Margaret," he said aloud. "Open the door, sweetheart."

As though hearing his plea, the door opened to reveal Margaret holding a crying Alison.

"Oh, Gib," Margaret said, her eyes filling with fresh tears.

Gib went into the house, shoved the door closed behind him and wrapped his arms around the miserable pair.

"Thank you," Margaret whispered, resting her head on his chest. "Thank you for coming, Gib. I was so frightened, because I was dizzy and couldn't take care of Alison the way I should." A sob caught in her throat. "I couldn't take care of my baby, Gib."

"Easy now," he said gently. "It's all right. Everything is going to be fine. You're sick? Both of you are ill?"

Margaret nodded. "The flu, I think. It came on so quickly. I'm worried about Alison getting dehydrated because she can't keep enough liquids down. I can't, either, but she's more important. Tend to Alison, please, Gibson."

Gib lifted Alison into his arms.

"Hi, kiddo," he said. "My Texas baby isn't feeling so good, huh?"

"Dough," Alison said, burying her face in Gib's neck. "Kitty."

Gib encircled Margaret's shoulders with his free arm.

"Let's get you into bed, Margaret."

"Alison needs juice, or even water. She—"

"Hey, you're dealing with a pro here, madam. I was the one who took over when Betsy was sick. Jell-O water. That's what's on the menu for our girl. I know all about this stuff. You just leave her to me and concentrate on yourself."

"But—"

"Shh. I'm running this show."

A short time later Margaret emerged from the bathroom clad in a pink cotton nightgown with eyelet trim. Her bed had been turned down and the fluffy pillow looked as if it had been delivered straight from heaven.

"In you go," Gib said, patting a fussing Alison on the back.

"Thank you," Margaret said, then sniffled. She crawled into bed and nestled her throbbing head on the cool pillow. "Oh, so lovely. I don't know how to thank you. I—"

"You've thanked me. Okay?" Gib drew the blankets over her. "Sleep."

"Mmm," Margaret said, her lashes drifting down.

"I love you, Margaret," Gib said quietly. "I am very much in love with you, and I love our Alison."

"Hmm?" Margaret said, not opening her eyes.

Gib leaned over and kissed her on the forehead.

"I love you," he whispered.

"I love you, too," she mumbled, "but don't tell Gib."

Gib straightened and stared down at Margaret with wide eyes. A grin broke across his face.

"I'll be damned," he said. "She loves me."

"Damned," Alison said, then threw up on Gib's shirt.

Margaret stirred, opened her eyes and immediately frowned. Her mind was a fuzzy blur of confusion, with scenes jumbled together in a maze.

She glanced at the clock and gasped as she saw it was 9:16 a.m.

"Alison," she said, sitting bolt right. "Gib," she added in the next instant.

Sinking back onto the pillow, she realized that her head no longer ached, her stomach was calm and her skin cool. Straining her ears, she heard no sounds coming from beyond her room.

She was going to check on Alison, she thought, but she needed a few seconds to sort through the muddle in her mind.

She and Alison had been hit by a fast-acting flu bug that obviously exited as quickly as it came.

It had been a horrible, frightening experience, the worst part being the knowledge that she was not physically capable of taking care of Alison.

And so she'd called Gib.

I'm on my way Gib had said. Nothing more, just *I'm on my way*, because she had told him that she needed him. And he'd come to her, without even asking why.

Like a knight on a white horse, he'd arrived and taken charge, scooping up Alison and tucking Margaret into bed.

"My hero," Margaret whispered, smiling.

But then she frowned again as she realized that something was nagging at her, that was just beyond her mental reach.

What was it? What...

"Oh," she said, her eyes widening as the remembrance slid into place.

I love you, Margaret. I am very much in love with you, and I love our Alison.

Margaret pressed trembling fingertips to her lips as Gib's words echoed over and over in her mind.

Gibson McKinley loved her? Was in love with her? Or had her feverish brain produced a dream where he'd said that? No, it was real. She was certain of it. She'd just gotten into bed, Gib had been holding Alison and—

"Good morning," Gib said from the bedroom doorway.

Margaret dropped her hands to the bed and looked at him. His hair was tousled, he had a dark stubble of beard and he was wearing a white T-shirt, although she could have sworn that he'd had on a red knit shirt last night.

"Hello," she said, attempting to smooth her hair.

Gib smiled. "You look lovely just as you are. Don't worry about your hair."

"I must see Alison," Margaret said, gripping the edge of the blanket to flip it back.

"Whoa," Gib said, raising one hand. "I know you want to check on her and you can...in a second. First comes my report. Alison is sleeping, making up some of the hours she lost last night."

"How is she?" Margaret said anxiously.

"Fit as a fiddle. She had a soft-boiled egg and toast fingers for breakfast, along with milk and apple juice. She ate every bite. Then I gave her a bath, and now she's snoozing. I'm doing a load of wash to take care of the soiled bed linens. Oh, and I'm washing my shirt. So! That's my report. Now it's your turn. How are you feeling?"

"I'm fine, I really am. I think I might even be hungry."

"A couple of people at *The Holler* have had this flu. It knocks you for a loop, but it doesn't last long. Why don't you look in on Alison, then I'll fix you some breakfast while you shower and dress?"

Margaret nodded. "Yes, all right." She paused. "Gib, I don't know what to say to you, how to thank you for all you've done. There just aren't enough words to express my gratitude."

"You thanked me enough times last night," he said, smiling. "You have credit stored up for several more of my dashes to the rescue."

"That's another thing, Gib. You came without even asking why I needed you here."

Gib's expression became serious. "I believe you

once said that was the measuring stick you used as to who was a true friend.''

"Yes."

Margaret forced herself to tear her gaze from Gib's. She threw back the blankets and left the bed.

"Alison," she said, hearing the unsteady thread of her voice.

"Your breakfast." Gib spun around and strode down the hall.

In Alison's room a soft smile formed on Margaret's lips as she stood by the crib. Alison was sleeping peacefully on her stomach, her thumb in her mouth. She was wearing a nightgown with pink and white angels sprinkled over the lightweight fabric.

Margaret touched the baby's forehead and found no evidence of a fever. After another lingering look at her daughter, Margaret headed for the shower.

It was unbelievable, Margaret thought as she made up the bed, how well she felt. It was as though she'd never been ill, except for feeling a little shaky from lack of food.

She finished smoothing the spread, then stood still, the delicious and tempting aroma of frying bacon reaching her.

She'd showered, shampooed and blow-dried her hair, applied light makeup and dressed in jeans and a blue cotton blouse. Sandals were on her feet, the bed was made, her nightgown was in the hamper.

There was nothing left to do to postpone going

into the kitchen where Gib was waiting for her, she thought.

Why was she so nervous about sitting across the breakfast table from him? He wasn't a stranger she hardly knew, for heaven's sake. He was Gibson McKinley.

Margaret sighed and frowned.

The man she loved.

The man who had declared his love for her in a voice husky with emotion.

She did not, she realized, like the idea of walking into her own kitchen and having no idea what was going to happen once she got there...beyond eating a piece of bacon.

Would Gib repeat his declaration of love? Or would he wait for her to bring up the subject of what he had said? And what did being in love mean to Gib? Would he once again broach the subject of their having an affair? Or...heavenly days...did being in love mean marriage, hearth and home to Gibson McKinley?

So many questions, Margaret thought, and hiding out in her bedroom wasn't going to enable her to get the answers she so desperately needed.

After taking a deep, steadying breath, she squared her shoulders and marched from the room.

"Perfect timing," Gib said when Margaret entered the kitchen. "Have a seat. Your breakfast is about to be served."

"Thank you," Margaret said, attempting and failing to produce a smile. "It smells delicious." She sat down at the table.

Gib set a plate of scrambled eggs, bacon and toast in front of Margaret, then filled two mugs with coffee and sat down opposite her.

"There you go," he said, placing a mug in front of Margaret's plate. "Are you still feeling all right?"

"Yes, just fine." Margaret spread her napkin on her lap and smoothed it with more attention than was necessary.

"Margaret?" Gib said quietly.

"Hmm?" she said, still fiddling with the napkin.

"Would you look at me, please?"

Margaret grabbed her fork, shoveled in a mouthful of eggs, then finally met Gib's gaze as she chewed. She raised her eyebrows questioningly.

"Do you remember what I said to you last night?" Gib said, looking directly into her eyes. "Did you hear me say that I love you? And that I love Alison?"

Margaret swallowed, the eggs feeling like marbles she was choking down.

"Yes," she whispered. "Yes, I heard you."

"Good. I meant it, Margaret, I truly did. I love you more than I can begin to even describe to you in words. You've given me so much, a whole new world of happiness I wasn't even aware was there. You and Alison are like precious gifts to be cherished, treasured, and I hope to do that."

"Oh" was all Margaret could say as the ache of unshed tears closed her throat.

She couldn't think straight! Gib was adding to the jumble in her brain, piling on more and more. There was just so much to attempt to deal with, *including* the knowledge that she was in love with him.

Gib frowned. "I wish I could just jump right in and propose to you, ask you to be my wife, my partner, for the remainder of our days. But I can't do that."

"You can't?"

"No, because things have suddenly become very complicated."

"They have?" Margaret said, feeling like an echoing idiot.

"Keep eating your breakfast. You need to regain your strength."

"For heaven's sake, Gib, how am I supposed to eat in the middle of a discussion like this?"

"Force yourself. Take a bite."

Margaret chomped on a piece of bacon, glaring at Gib at the same time. She took a sip of coffee, then plunked the mug back onto the table.

"All right," she said. "What is so complicated?"

"Benjamin."

Margaret opened her mouth, closed it, then tried again. "Benjamin?" she said, leaning slightly forward. "Benjamin? What does *that* baby have to do with what we're talking about?"

"I love Benny, Margaret," Gib said. "That little guy grabbed hold of my heart and won't let go." He paused. "This may sound corny, but Alison and Benjamin and, of course, my daughter, Betsy, own the father part of my heart. You own the section of my heart that is just a man."

Gib covered one of Margaret's hands with his on top of the table.

"Listen to me, Margaret, please. This is so important. I told Maggie how I felt about Benny. She gave me the name of the social worker handling his case."

"That is Patricia Conway. She was Alison's social worker, too."

"Yes. I telephoned Patricia and we talked at great length. Margaret, I'm going to start the paperwork to petition to adopt Benjamin."

"You're—" Margaret's eyes widened "—what?"

"Patricia said that Benny is definitely going to be put up for adoption, and that while I have strikes against me as an older, single father, it wasn't a hopeless endeavor on my part.

"Benjamin is considered a special-needs baby because he was addicted to drugs at birth. A great many people wouldn't even consider adopting him, because of the unknown long-range effects of the drugs."

"This is incredible," Margaret said, shaking her head. "I don't believe it. Well, yes, I believe it, but it's incredible. Good grief, I'm babbling. But, my gosh, Gib, I'm stunned."

"Margaret, do you understand now why I can't ask you to marry me?"

"I don't think I understand much of anything at the moment."

"Don't you see?" he said, his grip on her hand tightening. "My chances of being able to adopt Benjamin would be practically guaranteed if I was married to you. Since you have Alison, there would be no question in a judge's mind that you're prepared to raise a family again at your age."

"But..."

Gib got to his feet and began to pace back and forth beside the table. Margaret watched him intently, her heart racing and her mind whirling.

"If you agreed to marry me," Gib went on, "and there was the tiniest doubt in your mind regarding my intentions, that doubt would fester, grow and ultimately destroy us.

"Did I marry you because I truly love you? Or was it because you were the means by which I could have my son? If it wasn't for Benjamin, might I have asked you to be my lover, but not my wife? Those are the kinds of questions you could come to ask yourself."

Gib stopped his trek and looked at Margaret.

"I love you, Margaret Madison," he said, his voice thick with emotion. "I want you as my wife, my lover, my best friend. My love is real, and true and forever. But I have to know...*I have to be certain*...that you believe in that love, that there is no seed of doubt within you because of Benjamin."

Margaret pressed her fingertips to her temples.

"I can't digest all of this at once," she said.

"I realize that. You need time to sort it all through. I won't pester you, or do anything to attempt to sway your decision."

Margaret frowned. "Could you back up here a little? There seems to be a very big assumption on your part that my feelings for you match yours for me."

Gib smiled. "I know they do."

"Oh?" Margaret said, raising one eyebrow.

"Last night when I told you that I loved you, you said 'I love you, too.'" Gib chuckled. "Actually, you said, 'I love you, too, but don't tell Gib.'"

"Oh, heavens," Margaret said, feeling a flush of embarrassment warm her cheeks.

Gib's smile faded and his expression became serious again.

"I'm leaving now, Margaret," he said quietly. "God knows I don't want to go, but I have to in order to be fair to you, to give you time to think and reach a decision. It's up to you, all of it, the future, the... Well, enough said. I'll be waiting to hear from you."

Margaret just stared at him. Gib leaned over, kissed her gently on the forehead, then straightened.

"There's just one other thing," he said.

"Oh, why not?" Margaret said, flipping a hand in the air. "What's one more?"

"You know how Alison calls me a whole list of names?"

"Yes."

"Well, she finally figured it out in the middle of

the night. She picked the one she wanted and didn't call me anything other than that from then on.''

"Which name got her vote?" Margaret said wearily.

"Da-da.''

Chapter Fifteen

As Gib drove away from Margaret's home, each mile seemed like a hundred, creating a vast and dangerous distance between them.

Margaret alone, he thought, was a Margaret thinking, which was as it should be. But, oh, Lord, he wished he was still there with her, telling her over and over what a wonderful life they could have together, what a fantastic family they would all make. Telling her how much he truly loved her.

Gib, Margaret, Alison and Benjamin. Dad, Mom, daughter and son. The parents with the two terrific kids. The man and the woman, who would love each other totally, completely, until death parted them.

What a dynamite dream, Gib thought as he turned into his driveway. *Please* don't let it turn out to be just a pipe dream.

When Gib entered his living room he stood still in the silence that greeted him.

He was going to sell this house, he thought. Even if he ended up entirely alone, he couldn't live here anymore. If the judge allowed him to be Benjamin's father, he and his son would start fresh somewhere else.

And if Margaret trusted and believed in his love, and agreed to marry him, they'd decide together where they would live and raise their family. They would have a home overflowing with the sound of happy children's laughter.

Gib sighed, realizing he was tired after his night of being the doctor on duty. He'd sleep for a while, then concentrate on how he was going to hang on to his sanity while he was waiting for Margaret to reach the decision that would determine the course of his future.

"I love you, Margaret," Gib said aloud. "Oh, how I love you."

Margaret was so deep in thought that she looked down in surprise to see that she'd eaten her entire breakfast.

She pushed the plate to one side, propped an elbow on the table and rested her chin on her hand.

Her mind was a maze. She was chasing her own thoughts around like a hamster on a wheel that spun and spun but never went anywhere.

There was so much to deal with and she had to start someplace, or she'd go out of her mind.

Gibson McKinley was in love with her. She was in love with Gibson McKinley. *However,* because Gib wished to adopt Benjamin—which was incredible—there was room for doubt regarding Gib's motives for asking her to marry him.

Margaret blanked her mind and waited.

And waited.

She was mentally prepared to receive the chill, the arrival of the doubts.

But they never came.

A warmth suffused her and she straightened in the chair, a lovely smile, a woman-in-love smile, forming on her lips.

She believed in Gib's love, trusted it, because she trusted and believed in Gib himself. He was honest and real, a man of integrity, who had values that matched her own.

And Gib had come to her in the night because she'd said she needed him, and he hadn't asked why.

His arrival on her doorstep last night shouted the glorious message that their love was built on a foundation of friendship. Gibson was, indeed, her very best friend.

But marriage? Margaret thought. She'd never considered the possibility after Jack had died, and had certainly erased it completely from her mind when she'd adopted Alison.

But that was before Gib.

Mrs. Margaret Madison McKinley. Margaret McKinley. Mrs. Gibson McKinley. Wife of Gibson. Mother of Amy and Alison.

And Benjamin?

Oh, Benny, dear, sweet Benny, who looked so much like Gib it was uncanny. Benjamin, who might have now-unknown problems due to his birth mother's indulgence in drugs, difficulties that would simply be faced and handled if and when they materialized.

The buzzer on the clothes dryer shrilled, causing Margaret to jump in surprise. She got to her feet and went into the laundry room beyond the kitchen. Opening the dryer, she reached inside and pulled out the first article her hand touched.

It was Gib's red knit shirt.

Gripping it by the shoulders, Margaret shook it free of wrinkles, then held it at arm's length, envisioning how handsome Gib looked in the vibrant color.

"I love you, Gib," she said to the shirt. She laughed as the joy within her overflowed. Hugging the shirt to her breasts, she felt tears of happiness sting her eyes. "Yes, I'll marry you, Gibson McKinley. For better, for worse, in sickness and in health, and with two little ones in diapers, I'll marry you."

Early that evening Gib was slouched in his favorite chair, staring at a program on television that he wasn't paying the least bit of attention to.

It had been only hours since he'd left Margaret's, he thought glumly. Not years or months, weeks or days, only hours. Hours that added up to an eternity. He was *not* going to survive this.

There had to have been a better way to handle this, but for the life of him he couldn't think what it might have been. Margaret had to have time alone to think.

But, damn it, couldn't she think faster?

Easy, McKinley, he told himself. He was losing it. But, oh, man, what he wouldn't give to have Margaret Madison appear at his front door that very instant with a smile on her face, love in her heart and the word *yes* waiting to be spoken. He'd take her into his arms and...

The doorbell chimed, and Gib was so startled that he jumped to his feet, spun around and stared at the front door, his heart racing.

It was probably his neighbor returning the hedge trimmer he'd borrowed, Gib thought, stomping across the room. He'd nearly had a heart attack over a garden tool.

He flung the door open, then just stood there, not speaking, hardly breathing.

He'd lost his feeble mind, he thought frantically. He'd created a scenario in his head of Margaret arriving at his house, and now he was hallucinating, actually seeing the image of her there, instead of the neighbor with the hedge trimmer, who was really on his porch. He'd gone crazy!

"Gib? Am I disturbing you? Is this a bad time for you to have company?"

"Margaret?" Gib stepped closer. "Margaret? Is that really you?"

"Pardon me?" she said, obviously confused.

"Oh, cripe, come in, come in. I'm sorry. I was...never mind. It's a ridiculous story."

After Margaret entered the living room, Gib closed the door, then turned to look at her.

This was it, he thought. Margaret was here, and in the next few minutes he would know the verdict on his future happiness.

This was it, Margaret thought. She'd gathered her courage and here she was smack-dab in the middle of Gib's living room. The future of so many lives would be determined within the next few minutes.

"Please," Gib said with the sweep of one arm, "sit down. Would you like something to drink?"

"No, thank you."

"Where's Alison?"

"Justine is at the house taking care of her."

She crossed the room and sat down on the sofa. Gib followed and settled once again in his chair, leaning forward to look at Margaret intently.

"I'm returning your shirt," Margaret said, placing it on the cushion next to her.

"Margaret, if that's the only reason you're here, I'm going to pass out cold on the floor from stress. I realize that you have every right to take days, even weeks, to think about what I said to you this morning, but this has been one of the longest days of my life. Please tell me that you've reached a decision."

Margaret took a deep breath and lifted her chin. "I've reached a decision."

"Thank God," Gib muttered.

"Gib, I...I love you very much," Margaret said

softly. "I'm still rather stunned by that fact, because I never intended... What I mean is... Oh, drat, I'm a babbling wreck."

"You're doing fine. I love you, too, Margaret. I love you very, very much."

"Yes. Yes, I know you do. Gibson, you're not only the man I love, you're also my best friend. That's important, so very important. I have no doubts regarding your motives for asking me to marry you, because I believe in you, trust you, love you with all my heart."

Gib got to his feet slowly, his eyes never leaving Margaret's face.

"I would be happy to marry you, Gibson McKinley," she went on, "to have you be my husband, my partner in life and Alison's father. I also hope and pray that the court will allow us to adopt Benjamin. I...I accept your proposal of marriage."

Gib moved to stand in front of Margaret, and extended one hand to her. She placed her hand in his and he drew her up into his embrace.

"Thank you," he said, his voice husky with emotion. "Thank you."

Margaret smiled at him warmly. "You're welcome."

Then Gib lowered his head and kissed her.

It was a kiss of commitment, a pledge to a life together that would include two little children, who would look to them for love and guidance. It was a kiss of forever, until death parted them.

And it was a kiss of desire that exploded within them with hot, licking flames.

"I want you, Margaret," Gib murmured, close to her lips.

"I want you, too," she whispered.

Gib swung her up into his arms, and Margaret laughed in delight as he carried her across the room and down the hallway.

"My hero," she said. "This is just like in romantic movies."

"I'm in training, ma'am, for toting two little kids around."

In Gib's bedroom he set Margaret on her feet, swept back the blankets on the bed and turned on a small lamp, casting a golden glow over the room. He framed her face in his hands and looked directly into her eyes.

"I love you beyond measure," he said. "I am the happiest man alive."

"There are people who will think we're crazy for starting over with babies."

"Does it matter?"

"Not a bit. We're doing what's so very right for us, for our children. Oh, Gib, I do love you so much."

He captured her lips in a searing kiss, delving his tongue deep into her mouth to meet her tongue, stroking, dueling, as passions soared.

They ended the kiss reluctantly, then quickly shed their clothes, reaching for the other in the next instant. They tumbled onto the bed, lips meeting, hands caressing, bodies pressed close.

The want and need consuming them was ageless, as was their love. They were young and vibrantly alive; they were blessed with the wisdom of years that made them truly cherish what they had found together.

Gib drew the sweet flesh of one of Margaret's breasts into his mouth and she sighed in pure pleasure, her hands roaming over the taut muscles of his back. He moved to her other breast and she gasped from the building heat pulsing low within her.

"Gib, please."

He raised his head to look into her eyes. "Mrs. McKinley. My wife."

"Mr. McKinley. My husband."

"Forever."

And then he entered her and they were one entity. The tempo they set was thundering, wild, perfectly matched, beat for pounding beat. They were on fire, chasing the coveted summit, wanting it, needing it, reaching it at the same breathless moment. They were flung into oblivion and it was exquisite.

They lingered there, then floated back to reality. Gib shifted next to Margaret, sifting his fingers through her silken hair. She splayed one hand on his moist chest to feel the beating of his heart beneath her palm.

"Fantastic," Gib finally said.

"Wonderful," Margaret agreed.

"I wish you could spend the night, but I know you have to go home."

"Yes."

"We'll be married as soon as possible. All right? I want to wake up next to you in the mornings. We'll discuss where we'll live and all the other details, but let's get married soon."

"*Very* soon." Margaret laughed softly. "Poor Gib. You'll no longer qualify to be one of Houston's most eligible bachelors."

"That's fine with me."

"Well, if there is any doubt about your status in the minds of the female populace, I'll just quote our Texas baby."

"Oh?" Gib said, smiling. "And say what?"

"Mine!"

Their laughter mingled in the air, creating a joyous sound that would be part of every day of their lives. A sound that would fill the house where they chose to live, making it a warm and loving home.

Epilogue

"Oh, heavenly days, wasn't that somethin', that tale of true love comin' to Margaret and Gibson? 'Course, those Bishop boys were goin' 'round sayin' they knew all about it from way back when.

"Anyway, Margaret and Gibson got married, and I was there at the weddin'. I used up two hankies durin' the ceremony.

"They moved into Margaret's place and built on a family room. Then they got themselves a puppy that sweet little Alison calls Kitty, which is all right, 'cause the silly dog answers to it just fine.

"And then on a mighty special day, that fancy judge fella signed the papers that said Benjamin was to be a McKinley, too. Margaret, Gibson and Alison brought that baby home with 'em, which was exactly where he belonged.

"They're somethin' beautiful to behold, the four of 'em, when you see 'em together. It just goes to show that markin' years on a calendar doesn't mean a thing when it comes to lovin'.

"No, lovin' hearts don't grow older, they just grow bigger.

"And that's the truth of it, comin' straight from the heart of your Granny Bee."

Nancy and Tux Bishop
proudly and lovingly announce
the birth of their daughter
Sara Noel
on December 25

* * * * *

Coming this December 1997 from

Silhouette SPECIAL EDITION®

*AND BABY
MAKES THREE:
THE NEXT
GENERATION:*

*The Adams women of Texas
all find love—and
motherhood—in the most
unexpected ways!*

The Adams family of Texas returns!
Bestselling author **Sherryl Woods** continues
the saga in these irresistible new books.
Don't miss the first three titles in the series:

In December 1997: **THE LITTLEST ANGEL** (SE #1142)
When Angela Adams told Clint Brady she was pregnant, she
was decidedly displeased with the rancher's reaction. Could
Clint convince Angela he wanted them to be a family?

In February 1998: **NATURAL BORN TROUBLE** (SE #1156)
Dani Adams resisted when single dad Duke Jenkins claimed
she'd be the perfect mother for his sons. But Dani was
captivated by the boys—and their sexy father!

In May 1998: **UNEXPECTED MOMMY** (SE #1171)
To claim his share of the White Pines ranch, Chance Adams
tried to seduce his uncle's lovely stepdaughter. But then he
fell in love with Jenny Adams for real....

Available at your favorite retail outlet.

Silhouette®

Look us up on-line at: http://www.romance.net   SSE&BMTD-M

Take 4 bestselling love stories FREE

Plus get a FREE surprise gift!

Special Limited-time Offer

Mail to Silhouette Reader Service™

P.O. Box 609
Fort Erie, Ontario
L2A 5X3

YES! Please send me 4 free Silhouette Special Edition® novels and my free surprise gift. Then send me 6 brand-new novels every month, which I will receive months before they appear in bookstores. Bill me at the low price of $3.71 each plus 25¢ delivery and GST*. That's the complete price and a savings of over 10% off the cover prices—quite a bargain! I understand that accepting the books and gift places me under no obligation ever to buy any books. I can always return a shipment and cancel at any time. Even if I never buy another book from Silhouette, the 4 free books and the surprise gift are mine to keep forever.

335 BPA A3UZ

Name _____ (PLEASE PRINT)

Address _____ Apt. No. _____

City _____ Province _____ Postal Code _____

This offer is limited to one order per household and not valid to present Silhouette Special Edition® subscribers. *Terms and prices are subject to change without notice.
Canadian residents will be charged applicable provincial taxes and GST.

CSPE-696   ©1990 Harlequin Enterprises Limited

Welcome to the Towers!

In January
New York Times bestselling author

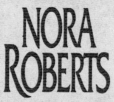

NORA ROBERTS

takes us to the fabulous Maine coast mansion
haunted by a generations-old secret and introduces
us to the fascinating family that lives there.

Mechanic Catherine "C.C." Calhoun and hotel magnate
Trenton St. James mix like axle grease and mineral
water—until they kiss. Efficient Amanda Calhoun finds
easygoing Sloan O'Riley insufferable—and irresistible.
And they all must race to solve the mystery
surrounding a priceless hidden emerald necklace.

Catherine and Amanda

THE Calhoun Women

**A special 2-in-1 edition containing
COURTING CATHERINE and A MAN FOR AMANDA.**

Look for the next installment of
THE CALHOUN WOMEN with Lilah and Suzanna's
stories, coming in March 1998.

Available at your favorite retail outlet.

▼ *Silhouette*®

Look us up on-line at: http://www.romance.net   CWVOL1

SILHOUETTE WOMEN KNOW ROMANCE WHEN THEY SEE IT.

And they'll see it on **ROMANCE CLASSICS**, the new 24-hour TV channel devoted to romantic movies and original programs like the special **Romantically Speaking—Harlequin™ Goes Prime Time**.

Romantically Speaking—Harlequin™ Goes Prime Time introduces you to many of your favorite romance authors in a program developed exclusively for Harlequin® and Silhouette® readers.

Watch for **Romantically Speaking—Harlequin™ Goes Prime Time** beginning in the summer of 1997.

If you're not receiving ROMANCE CLASSICS, call your local cable operator or satellite provider and ask for it today!

ROMANCE CLASSICS

Escape to the network of your dreams.

See Ingrid Bergman and Gregory Peck in *Spellbound* on Romance Classics.

©1997 American Movie Classics Co. "Romance Classics" is a service mark of American Movie Classics Co. Harlequin is a trademark of Harlequin Enterprises Ltd. Silhouette is a registered trademark of Harlequin Books, S.A.

RMCLS-S-R2

As seen on TV!
Free Gift Offer

With a Free Gift proof-of-purchase from any Silhouette® book, you can receive a beautiful cubic zirconia pendant.

This gorgeous marquise-shaped stone is a genuine cubic zirconia—accented by an 18" gold tone necklace.

(Approximate retail value $19.95)

Send for yours today…
compliments of ▼ *Silhouette*®
™

To receive your free gift, a cubic zirconia pendant, send us one original proof-of-purchase, photocopies not accepted, from the back of any Silhouette Romance™, Silhouette Desire®, Silhouette Special Edition®, Silhouette Intimate Moments® or Silhouette Yours Truly™ title available at your favorite retail outlet, together with the Free Gift Certificate, plus a check or money order for $1.65 U.S./$2.15 CAN. (do not send cash) to cover postage and handling, payable to Silhouette Free Gift Offer. We will send you the specified gift. Allow 6 to 8 weeks for delivery. Offer good until December 31, 1997, or while quantities last. Offer valid in the U.S. and Canada only.

Free Gift Certificate

Name: _____

Address: _____

City: _____ State/Province: _____ Zip/Postal Code: _____

Mail this certificate, one proof-of-purchase and a check or money order for postage and handling to: SILHOUETTE FREE GIFT OFFER 1997. In the U.S.: 3010 Walden Avenue, P.O. Box 9077, Buffalo NY 14269-9077. In Canada: P.O. Box 613, Fort Erie, Ontario L2Z 5X3.

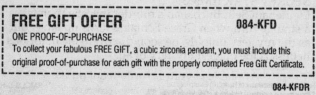

FREE GIFT OFFER
ONE PROOF-OF-PURCHASE
To collect your fabulous FREE GIFT, a cubic zirconia pendant, you must include this original proof-of-purchase for each gift with the properly completed Free Gift Certificate.

084-KFD

084-KFDR

The Stars of Mithra

**Three gems,
three beauties,
three passions...
the adventure of a lifetime**

SILHOUETTE·INTIMATE·MOMENTS®
brings you a thrilling new series by
New York Times bestselling author

Nora Roberts

**Three mystical blue diamonds place three close
friends in jeopardy...and lead them to romance.**

In October
HIDDEN STAR (IM#811)
Bailey James can't remember a thing, but she knows
she's in big trouble. And she desperately needs private
investigator Cade Parris to help her live long enough to
find out just what kind.

In December
CAPTIVE STAR (IM#823)
Cynical bounty hunter Jack Dakota and spitfire
M. J. O'Leary are handcuffed together and on the run
from a pair of hired killers. And Jack wants to know
why—but M.J.'s not talking.

In February
SECRET STAR (IM#835)
Lieutenant Seth Buchanan's murder investigation takes
a strange turn when Grace Fontaine turns up alive. But
as the mystery unfolds, he soon discovers the notorious
heiress is the biggest mystery of all.

Available at your favorite retail outlet.

Look us up on-line at: http://www.romance.net   MITHRA